SOMEONE TO RESCUE

BY DALE DAVIS

Table of Contents

Chapter 1
Surprise Encounter

Blake Patterson was the type of person every boy in high school wanted to be like, and every girl wanted to date. He was 6'2", broad-shouldered, had thick, dark, curly hair, and a deep, staccato voice. He usually wore blue jeans and a black t-shirt, but when it was cold he sported his letterman's jacket that he had earned playing varsity football since his freshman year. He often carried around a football even when it wasn't football season. Despite the fact that he was the most popular kid in school, he always seemed friendly to everyone, even the 'undesirables.' I still remember my first unexpected encounter with him on a late afternoon during my senior year.

"Do you need help with that?" Blake asked me as I struggled to carry my books, backpack, lunch bag, and binder, all while trying to text my parents that I would be home late from school.

"That would be great," I replied before I even knew who had spoken. I looked up and was startled when I realized that it was Blake. This was the first time I had ever met Blake and although I knew his reputation for being friendly, I had never really thought that extended to "undesirables" like me.

Even though I was a senior in high school, I was only 5'2" and skinny as a thin, tall snake. Many girls at school were thin like me, but most were only thin where it counted. I was thin all over. My Mom always said, "Elizabeth, you'll come into your own soon enough," whatever that meant. I wore glasses with thick lenses and had acne that made my face look like an advertisement for the Braille community. Over the previous summer, I had gotten contacts after begging my parents relentlessly for weeks, and my zits had cleared up so that I was almost unrecognizable from the nerdy squirt of the previous year everyone enjoyed making fun of. I was still an "undesirable" because I was part of the crowd that cared more about studying than football scores. I had a couple of friends, but they also cared less about what popular kids wore and more about what test scores they got on their algebra tests. I always got A's. Once, I got an A- and it bugged me so much that I stayed in the library all the next week and studied. I even skipped lunches that week and brushed up on quadratic equations regardless of the fact that I knew they would probably not be on the test.

I was startled beyond belief when Blake grabbed half my books and said, "You're Beth, right?" Nobody called me Beth, but he smiled when he said this and my heart suddenly started beating so hard that I could feel it pulsing through my whole body, so I kind of forgot what my name was. I was sure my heart was beating so loudly that Blake could hear it.

At first, I didn't say anything. I just stared dumbfounded at his gray-blue eyes peering out from under his dark, curly hair. Finally, I managed a shaky "Um, yeah."

Blake looked back at me with a nervous smile. What did he have to be nervous about, I wondered. I struggled to try to think of something to say that would make an impression on him other than, "What a weirdo," which I imagined he must be thinking. I could think of nothing, and it was as if my head was full of cotton balls, and my normal quick wit was as slow as molasses. Blake didn't seem to mind. We just walked along in silence.

After a while, I remembered that I couldn't just walk aimlessly throughout eternity with this hunk of a boy next to me and started worrying about where I should go. I had been on my way home, but my home wasn't exactly what I would want Blake--or anyone else for that matter--to see. It was a 1930s two-story, wood-sided retro house that wasn't impressive even when it was first built. The once-white exterior was yellowed and peeling as if it had sat in the rain and baked in the hot sun for too many years, which it had.

I was never really embarrassed by where I lived, but I never invited friends over--even my best friend, Rebecca--and certainly had never imagined having someone like Blake see it. It wasn't that we were poor. My dad had a good job, one at which he worked far too many hours, but ever since my mom had quit her job to become a stay-at-home mom, we had to watch our spending. We always had enough, but never enough to splurge on things like house paint.

He seemed to notice my hesitation and spoke first. "I noticed you spend a lot of time in the library. Were you on your way there to study?"

"Sure," I muttered. What was happening? How could Blake know I spent so much time in the library? Could he actually have noticed me? Could this be a prank? Maybe his friends put him up to this. My mind raced with the possibilities as we walked toward the school library. I turned and looked at him out of the corner of my eyes as we approached the library. He looked very somber as if he had something terrible on his mind, but didn't want to let anyone know.

Finally, we reached the steps to the library. Normally, this was where I felt comfortable and safest. This was my realm. As we walked up the steps I still had a jittery feeling in my throat that reached all the way down to my stomach. I felt excited but scared. If I tried to talk, I might throw up. That would be just like me. I didn't know what to do, so I just kept quiet. I do quiet really well. Sometimes I can have a whole conversation with my friends without saying anything. I just listen while they prattle on.

Blake had a nervous, crooked smile as he handed me my books. What did he have to be nervous about? "Well, good luck with whatever you're studying for, Beth." He looked like he wanted to say more but wasn't sure. I'd always assumed popular kids like Blake were self-assured. His eyes held a sadness I hadn't noticed before. What could he have to be sad about, I wondered. He had everything, friends, popularity, looks…

I said goodbye and wondered if I would see Blake again on Monday after the weekend. I wondered if he would ignore me if his friends were around or if he would be just as genuine as he seemed to be that day. I wondered what he was thinking and what he really seemed to want to talk about. His eyes seemed so solemn. On the walk to my car all I could think about was how he seemed nervous and smiled when he said goodbye. That smile sustained me throughout the whole weekend.

Normally, I spend most of Saturday alone in my room studying even though I don't really have any homework on weekends. That Saturday, I might as well not even have cracked open a book. I know I must have studied, but in reality, I spent the whole weekend daydreaming about how our hands briefly touched when he grabbed my books.

By Monday, I had come back to reality and came to the realization that I had wasted the whole weekend conjuring up scenarios that were pure fantasy. Blake would probably not even remember me, and I was sure he had not even given our brief encounter a second thought--probably forgetting it as he walked away. Still, as I trudged through the day, I had to admit to myself that I was uncharacteristically distracted. Every time I turned a corner or came out of a building, I caught myself looking around. It wasn't until lunchtime that I admitted to myself that I was looking for Blake. I also admitted to myself that I was unlikely to see him and that even if I did see him, he would probably be with his friends and would not even remember me.

The last bell rang, and I left my seventh period in a melancholy mood. I knew I was being ridiculous, but I couldn't help myself. I decided to treat myself to an extra hour of studying in the library. I didn't really have any homework since I had done it all in class, but often, when I was a little down, I could always take my mind off any perceived problems by spending time in the library with math drills, science reckonings, or light Shakespeare reading.

As I left my seventh-period class, I walked across the grassy Quad toward the library. The grass was tall and tickled my bare ankles since I was wearing tennis shoes with no socks and the school didn't regularly mow the Quad because there always seemed to be students hanging out. The Quad seemed like the perfect hangout spot for many students. It was surrounded by the science building on the west, the drama and performing arts building on the south, and on the east side of the Quad was what used to be the vocation-ed building where students had been able to learn woodworking, auto mechanics, metal shop, and auto body--until those subjects had been scrapped for more test-boosting subjects like math intervention and enrichment. There were concrete benches where students could sit and talk or make out, plenty of grass where students could sit and eat, read, or talk, and sometimes there were even people throwing around a frisbee or football. I preferred the solitude of the library.

The library was more isolated and private because even though it was open until 4:30 on weekdays, very few students ever went to the library after school. Usually, I had the place nearly to myself, especially on Friday afternoons. Occasionally, there were a few kids from the Chess Club using one of the conference rooms to play Skittles, but they were always quiet and statue-like as they stared at their boards.

The library had marble steps going up to a set of big wooden doors that had designs carved into them. It looked like a building from the 1800s, and I loved everything about it. It always smelled like a combination of old books and cleaning solution--kind of like paper and soap.

My mom was an office assistant, and she said when she started working, she used what was called a ditto machine. And she said when they switched to copy machines, she missed the smell of the ditto machines the most. She described the smell as a combination of ink and vanilla. For me, the library is probably my favorite smell in the world. I know that sounds weird, but the library sometimes felt more like home to me than home did.

Sometimes, I felt like the Henry Bemus character in that old *Twilight Zone* TV show episode where the whole world is destroyed and he is just about to end his life when he finds a library. It didn't end well for him, but still, the library saved his life. Like him, reading is my favorite thing to do. I don't know what I would do without reading.

I was about ten feet from the steps and carrying all my books, backpack, purse, and binder--as usual--when I heard a voice behind me. "Need help with that?"

I froze for a moment, and my insides felt like I had swallowed a whole popsicle and gotten it stuck halfway down my throat. I knew it was Blake before I even turned around. "Sure, that would be great," I replied. Somehow, I got the words out without stammering, but my face felt hot, as if it was badly sunburned. I wondered if my cheeks were blushing red or if they had drained of all color and were pale.

Blake didn't seem to notice anything out of the ordinary. He just grabbed my books, leaving me with only my binder, backpack, and purse. He started walking and was already a couple of steps away from me when I remembered to start walking, too.

Blake was wearing faded blue jeans, a tight black T-shirt, and old checkered Vans. His wavy dark hair looked like he had just had it styled at a salon, and showed no signs of having worn a helmet for football practice. I wondered if football had started yet. I didn't really keep up with trivial things that the rest of the school seemed so obsessed about. Blake managed to carry all my books in one arm and still have room while holding a football in his left hand.

"Don't tell me you have a lot of homework already. We just came back from the weekend. What teacher assigns a bunch of homework on Saturday and Sunday?"

"I don't really have homework," I admitted. "I just like getting ahead."

I expected him to laugh or crack a joke, but instead, he just looked at me and gave me that nervous smile he had. As we walked the last few steps to the library, I forced myself to focus on taking one step at a time carefully so I wouldn't trip over myself. My heart was pounding in my chest, and I could feel my pulse in my neck. I wondered if Blake could hear it. I silently chastised myself for being silly and tried to think about something else. I silently started doing math equations in my head to calm myself, but I couldn't even focus on that, so I finally gave up.

"So, what brings you here?" I asked because I couldn't think of anything else to say and the silence was starting to get awkward. I've noticed that there are two types of people. Some people are comfortable with silence, while others turn into chatterboxes whenever there's a lull. I'm the latter, and the longer the silence, the more words seem to bottle up and want to bubble out of me.

"When there's no practice, I usually stay at school for a while because I don't really like to go home right away," he replied. That brought up more questions in me than answers, but I was afraid to say more, fearing it would offend him or break whatever imaginary connection I had conjured up in my mind.

We got to the library steps in seconds, although it seemed like it stretched out longer. Time is funny that way. Sometimes, it seems to go by quickly and events blur together, and other times, it slows down. I never know what it's going to do or why it does either.

When he handed my books back, I took a deep breath, slowly inhaled deeply, and held it. Blake had a clean soap smell to him mixed with some floral smell-- probably from whatever conditioner he used to get his hair to look like it did--leather and maybe the smell of cedar wood. I couldn't quite place it. It was uniquely pleasant but somehow not what I expected. He didn't smell like I thought a football player would, but he still managed to have a very masculine smell. "Well, see you around, Beth," and just like that, he turned and walked away, and the encounter was over again.

I'd like to say I really studied over the next couple of hours in the library, but the truth is, I don't remember anything I read, and after only 30 minutes, I gave up and left. When I walked back down the library steps, I looked around expectantly, just in case Blake was still around. I knew I was being silly, but I also knew I wasn't going to be able to stop myself.

The next morning, I woke up feeling the warm comforter pulled up under my chin. I had gone to bed early but still slept past my usual 5 A.M. wake-up time. Even though school didn't start until 8:05, I always liked to get to school early, so I didn't feel rushed and so that I could plan out my day and think about what assignments I might have. I was determined to put any foolishness aside and get back into my regular, comfortable routine.

By a quarter to 6, I was sitting at the kitchen table with a bowl of cereal, half Frosted Flakes, half Raisin Bran. It was obvious that Mom hadn't gone to the store this week.

I enjoy getting up before anyone else so I can have some quiet time to myself in the morning. I usually eat breakfast, look ahead in my math, history, science, or English books to see what assignments are coming up, and just enjoy the sugar rush that my cereal and sugary milk bring. I was just drinking the sweet milk from my bowl when my mom came into the kitchen, dressed like she had a full day of work--downtown.

Even though she's a stay-at-home mom, she usually is up early and dressed like she is going to work in a law office, which is where she used to work before she decided to stay home and "take care of me." Like I needed taking care of. When she left her office job the whole office threw her a party and said they wouldn't be able to get along without her. I know because she brought me to work on her last day. It was supposed to be some kind of lesson for me, although I don't know what it was I was supposed to learn--something about the people behind the scenes being important too. I was in 6th grade at the time, but I was already going into advanced classes, and my mom thought she'd take a break so she "could be there for me if I needed her." Obviously, I don't need her, but it is nice to have her around more. She always gets up to see me off to school, and normally, she sits with me during breakfast to talk and see what's going on in my life, which is usually nothing.

I wondered what she would say if I told her I met a boy. I know it would be stretching the truth to near infinity, but it would be fun just to see her reaction. Mom has been waiting for me to go boy-crazy since I was in junior high. It's funny, but when I ask her what she was like in junior high, she just says, "A lot like you." She sure didn't dress like me. Today, she wore black slacks, a cream-colored blouse with pale pink roses over it, and a black suit jacket. Her long, dark hair was in a bun, which is how she normally wore it. She had horned-rimmed glasses like I used to wear before I got contacts.

"Good morning, Elizabeth. How's your day going?"

"Well, it just started, but so far, so good," I replied. A lot of kids that I know don't get along well with their parents, but I've always had a pretty good relationship with both my mom and dad. I guess I'm lucky that way.

"Got any plans for the rest of the week?" she asked.

"I thought I'd fly to London and then to Paris," I joked. "I hear the weather is perfect right now." Mom laughed quietly, and that's one thing I like about her. Even though my jokes aren't that funny, she still laughs like they really amuse her. "Anyway, I'll probably just go to the library after school."

"You know, there's more to life than studying."

"Believe me, I know," I replied, thinking about the possibility of seeing Blake again.

"What's that mean?" she probed.

"Uh, nothing," I replied, hoping my quick response didn't give away the fact that I was letting my imagination run wild.

I finished breakfast and left Mom sitting at the breakfast table, drinking her coffee and working on a crossword puzzle. I grabbed my backpack and car keys and headed out the door. I threw my backpack into the passenger seat of my blue Honda Civic.

My parents had "surprised" me with this car over the summer. It wasn't much of a surprise since it was my mom's old car. She got a new one for her birthday, even though she hardly drives anywhere now. At the time, I figured the Civic would pass down to me, and a couple of months later, on July 4, which was my birthday, I found out I was right. It's not a flashy car, but I liked it because it meant I wouldn't have to ride the bus anymore. Dad liked it because it was a "safe, dependable automobile." Anyway, even though it was 10 years old, it still ran great, and the grayish-blue paint still looked good, with only a couple of door dings in it.

As I drove to school, I still had to concentrate on driving. I got my license over a year before, but I still hadn't driven enough to be able to drive without thinking about what I was doing. Since I got the Honda over the summer, this was the first year I was driving to school instead of riding the bus.

I was excited for the day, but I'm the weirdo kid who actually likes school so I always enjoy the drive to school. I pulled into the student parking lot to see that there was only one other car, a black Audi TTS that I knew belonged to my friend, Rebecca. Even though it wasn't really a contest, we both knew that we each tried to beat the other one to school each morning. Sometimes, I got here so early it was ridiculous.

I knew she would be sitting outside the student store even though it didn't open until 7:30. Rebecca always started her day with a Coke, and a bag of chips from home, and a shortbread cookie from the student store. On Fridays she would have two cookies if she deemed it an especially difficult week. She was sitting on a concrete bench with a book open and her backpack next to her.

She was wearing a Frogger t-shirt, jean shorts, and heavy black boots. I think she always wore boots to add an inch or two to her height. Even still, she was very short, and I knew she was as touchy about her height as she was about her weight. She exploded whenever someone made fun of her height or weight, so of course, many did just that to see her reaction. Her hair was dark brown with faded purple-dyed streaks mixed throughout. She didn't look like a nerd, except that she always had her nose in a book, like she did right now.

"Hey, Rebecca. What's new?" I asked.

I sat down beside her and pulled out my science book to look over the material for today. Mrs. Hart always liked to spring "surprise" quizzes on Mondays, but sometimes she would wait a day and give them on Tuesdays. She hadn't given a "surprise" test yesterday, so I figured we were due. Rebecca didn't look up from her book right away but kept reading and finally put a plump finger on the page and looked up. "Hey, Elizabeth. Have you ever read *The Vampire Diaries*? It's really good."

"Didn't you read that last year? I remember you asking me about it before."

"I read it every year. It's really good," she explained. "Plus, it's informative. You know vampires are real. People think they're just a myth, but they were based on a real story, and there are thousands of people who disappear every year. Where do you think those people go?" She looked at my science book with suspicion. "Not everything can be explained with 'Science,'" she explained.

It's nice to have a predictable friend. I always know what she's going to say, even if it's sometimes a little crazy, and if I need to talk to somebody, I usually always know where she'll be. She was a creature of habit. It was kind of comforting to have someone so dependable. It was true she did have some beliefs that were very outlandish, like UFOs, chupacabra, ghosts, and vampires. It was weird to me that someone who was so smart could believe in so many myths, but then she did get a B in chemistry last year so she wasn't infallible. She also believed every government conspiracy theory she ever heard, but deep down, she was dependable and always there for me.

"I'm more of a *Lorna Doone* or even *Harry Potter* kind of person, but maybe I'll give it a try sometime," I replied.

She offered me some chips, but I said I wasn't hungry. She ate a few as she went back to her book. She kept reading while we talked about different classes, teachers, and assignments. She paused her reading for a moment and asked, "Are you going to the game on Friday?"

"What game?" I asked.

"Duh…the football game. You *never* come." Rebecca always went to football games even though she knew nothing about football--but then again, I knew less than she did.

Rebecca was always going to rallies and dances and games and trying to fit in. On Mondays, she would usually talk about how fun they were, but I knew she was probably alone in the bleachers. She would talk about what songs were played at the dances but would never talk about anyone she danced with, and I knew she probably never got asked to dance. My feelings were always split. I felt guilty for leaving her to be alone at events like that, but I didn't want to spend a whole evening alone with her, watching others have fun.

"I don't know. I guess we'll see," I answered. I always said that just like my mom always said that when she meant no. I couldn't see myself going to a football game or a dance and just standing around looking at everyone else and having fun. I would rather shove pins under my fingernails.

"I'd be a lot safer in the parking lot if I didn't have to walk alone," she replied as if that explained anything. She could still be talking about vampires, but she could just as easily be talking about Hanna Cranna, the witch of Monroe County. She was always telling me about some new beast she had read about, and it didn't matter how fantastic and unbelievable, or even like Hanna Cranna, if it was from a completely different area like Connecticut, which is nowhere close to where we live. I was never sure if she actually believed everything or if some of the time she was putting me on, but I did know she did seem to believe a lot of it.

"Yeah," I grunted, "I think I have something to do Friday."

"Yeah, right," she said. "You never do anything but study."

"I'm hurt that you would think that," I responded, knowing that she was probably right.

"Well, don't worry. On Monday, I'll tell you what you missed."

I felt guilty that she was disappointed, but I wasn't feeling guilty enough to change my mind. Usually, I waited with Rebecca until the student store opened, and we walked over to the library to read or hang out before our first class started, but I was feeling a lot of awkwardness, so I decided not to wait. "Do you want to go hang out by the library?" I asked, knowing she would wait for her cookie. "I'm going to wait for it to open."

"No, I'm good. I'm going to wait for the student store to open and see what they have." I caught myself smiling. She almost always said she would "see what they have," as if she didn't buy a shortbread cookie every single day. I wondered what she would do after she graduated from high school. Would she swing by here on her way to college to pick up a shortbread cookie? I smiled again as I pictured her in my imagination 10 years from now, still visiting the high school student store to get her shortbread cookie.

"Plus, it's daylight, so I'll be okay. I'll meet you later," she threw in. Sometimes I wondered why all my friends seemed so weird and wondered if I was just as weird and I just didn't realize it because only others looking from outside my bubble could see it.

I walked across the slightly wet grass of the Quad on my way to the library. The smell of the grass reminded me of the hay barn at my grandparents' house in Lawrence, Kansas. We used to visit them every summer until my grandpa passed away, and my grandma had to sell the farm and move into a senior assisted living center. My mom usually still went to visit two or three times a year still, but I seldom went anymore because she went during the school year. She always said Grandma was doing great, but she always came back in a gloomy mood.

I was just passing the science and economics building, Kennedy Center, when I heard a voice from my left call out to me. "Hey, Beth." I turned to see where the voice was coming from and, more importantly, who it could be coming from since the only person I knew who was ever here this early was back at the cookie line where I left her. Blake was walking straight toward me, and suddenly, my mind went blank. My feet stopped dead in their tracks like they were glued to the pavement.

He walked right up to me and grabbed my stack of books. "Don't tell me you're going to the library this early," he said. "It doesn't even open until 7:30."

He was wearing his normal black T-shirt, faded blue jeans, and checkered Vans. His dark curly hair was catching the morning sun, and I could just catch a scent of a clean soap smell and some type of fruity condition or shampoo--that I thought I had imagined the last time we had met--mixed with the smell of leather and definitely cedar wood this time--or maybe it was sandalwood.

I wasn't sure what to say, or even how to talk, or even how to breathe. "Hey, Blake," I finally managed. "Yeah, no, I was just going to sit on the steps until it opened."

"Mind if I sit with you?" he asked. Before I could answer, he sat down on the white marble steps. The steps were at least 6' wide, but he sat just inches from me. I drew in a breath, trying to think of something to say. Usually, I'm a chatterbox, but for some reason, I couldn't think of anything but the light smell of soap and some type of fruity or flowery conditioner, maybe gardenias or honeysuckle, mixed with the odors of wood and leather.

"You come early," he said, breaking the silence. "Especially since it's only Monday, and we just had two days off."

"Uh, yeah. I like to read or study before classes," I faltered. I couldn't think of anything else to say, so I just looked down at my hands, which were gripping each other so hard they were turning white. I forced myself to relax my hands and suddenly wished I hadn't eaten breakfast because, out of nowhere, I felt like I was going to throw up. I didn't remember ever being nervous like this before. I am usually the first to volunteer for presentations in class, and I even enjoy speaking in front of the class.

"I try to get out of the house before my dad wakes up," Blake said. "Usually, he wakes up pretty late, but once in a while, he manages to rouse himself before I'm gone, and he's usually in a pretty foul mood no matter what time it is or who's around."

I didn't know how to respond, so I said, "I bet your mom isn't happy about that."

His facial expression changed, and I could tell I had said something wrong. "My mom…" he hesitated as if not sure what to say. His face looked pale but somehow his neck looked darker reddish-purple, as if all the color went from his face to his neck, "...left us a few years ago," he finished.

"I'm so sorry," I replied. Again, I didn't really know what to say. Weird how I was always the one with the answers, the one who could always talk about anything, yet now my brain was like an empty sack of air.

We both sat on the cool bench for a couple of minutes, neither one talking. I was torn between staying silent and asking more questions like why is he talking to me, what can I say to make him feel better, or think I'm not a bonehead.

After a couple of minutes that felt like 30, he said, "Yeah. There are lots of times when I wish I could go be with her, but it's okay. I don't talk about it much and people don't ask me about much of anything except football. It's like they think that's all I am. Sometimes I feel like I'm invisible. Nobody can see the real me. All they see is a football player jock. There's a real person inside, but nobody wants to take any time to find out about me."

Again, the silence lingered. I was thinking that this might be the longest I'd been quiet since I was a baby. I wanted to say something, but I just couldn't think of anything. Finally, I had to say something because the unwieldiness between us was torture. "People probably just admire how good you are. It must be great to be so good at something."

He looked up at me, and his gray-blue eyes seemed to look deep inside of me. "You're like the smartest kid in school, aren't you?" he said. "Everyone knows you're like the best at anything school-related." Then he smiled a crooked kind of smile again, and although he looked like he was the happiest person in the world, I could tell it was a mask he put on for others.

Unexpectedly and without thinking, I said, "It must be a lot tougher to be you than most people realize." After I said it, I wondered where it had come from. It's not like I was a very deep person or anything like that.

"Wow, I knew you were smart, Beth, but you're probably the only person in my life who understands me."

Those words strangely comforted me while confusing me at the same time. I was in his life? How weird to think that he had said that to me when we really didn't know each other. I began to wonder what he meant. Did he just throw that out to say something to break the silence? Was this part of his mask? Did he really have nobody in his life that he could talk to and so he felt truly alone? Was he just making fun of me and all this was some joke or prank. I looked at his eyes to try to figure out what was going through his mind. I could tell he was sincere.

Somehow I knew that he had meant it. "Thanks," I mumbled.

"Hey are you going to the game on Friday?"

"Of course," I said, not knowing what else to say.

"Well, sit on the west side. That's where we come out. Maybe we can go to the dance or hang out after the game. Blake stood up and held out my books. "Thanks again, Beth," he said. I should be thanking him. Before I could think of how to reply he said, "It was nice having someone to talk to for a change. Usually, I just hang out and walk around campus alone." At this time I wasn't thinking about classes, tests, books, or anything else. Usually, it's all I think about, but right then, I probably couldn't have remembered what my first period class was.

I grabbed my books and meekly stammered, "Yeah, it was nice," immediately chastising myself for not saying something smarter.

"Good morning, Elizabeth," Mrs. Young called out. "Good morning, young man." I was surprised she didn't know Blake's name. Everyone knew Blake. While it was true that Mrs. Young had probably never been to a football game, neither had I, and I knew who Blake was.

I knew Mrs. Young probably spent almost all her time in the library checking books in or out and putting them back on the shelves. I don't know how long she had been the librarian, but my mom said that she was the librarian when she had gone to school there. Mrs. Young looked like she was at least 80. She usually wore a flower-printed dress that looked like it was from the 1800's. Her glasses had a little chain on the frames that went around her neck for when she took them off, which I had never seen her do. She was paper thin and looked like a strong breeze would blow her over. Her skin was kind of a transparent grayish-tan that reminded me of Play-Doh that had been left out too long. She always had a smile, although her teeth looked like dentures.

I had spent so much time over the last three years in the library that she definitely knew me although often she called me by the wrong name. I wondered if she remembered my mom. My mom said she used to spend a lot of time in the library when she was my age.

Blake stood up and held out my books. "Thanks again, Beth," he said. I should be thanking him. Before I could think of how to reply he said, "It was nice having someone to talk to for a change. Usually, I just hang out and walk around campus alone." At this time I wasn't thinking about classes, tests, books, or anything else. Usually, it's all I think about, but right then, I probably couldn't have remembered what my first period class was.

I grabbed my books and meekly stammered, "Yeah, it was nice," immediately chastising myself for not saying something smarter.

Now as I began replaying our conversation back through my mind, I seriously wondered how I would know if I had said something wrong or made a mistake. I had no way of knowing what I was supposed to say or do in social situations like this. I couldn't even fathom why Blake had approached me in the first place. Thinking back, there was a moment when he seemed moderately vulnerable and seemed to open up more than someone with whom you had just met would typically do. This, above all, calmed me and made me feel like I could trust Blake. I couldn't really say why, but there was something innocent and childlike about him that seemed unguarded and exposed.

Maybe I had just imagined it and I was reading too much into it. Still, he did ask me if I'd be at the game and I was pretty sure he had asked me out afterwards. Me. I couldn't fathom it. He had said I was the only person in the world who understood him. How could that be when I barely knew him? Was he that alone? I dismissed that thought immediately. That couldn't be it. He was probably the most popular kid at school. He must have loads of friends.

Still, there had seemed to be a moment when I mentioned his mom, and a shadow of pain had flickered across his face before he had put a smile back on. It had seemed like he had let his mask slip for a brief moment and had let me glimpse some part of a private world that he usually kept locked away. The question I kept asking myself was, why me? I was nothing special. Did he truly have no one else?

I kept replaying our conversation over and over again. I reached the sidewalk on the other side of the quad before I knew it. I didn't even remember walking across the grass. Abruptly, Rebecca was right beside me.

"Elizabeth? Didn't you hear me calling you?" asked Rebecca. "You kept walking and just ignored me," she admonished.

I broke out of my reverie. "Yeah, no. Sorry. I didn't hear you," I said. "I was thinking about science class. Do you think we'll have a test today?" If I had one person in the world that I could trust any secret with--if I had any--it would be Rebecca. Still, I didn't feel comfortable sharing what had happened between Blake and me. I didn't even know what had happened between Blake and me. If anything had even happened--or would be happening--I didn't want to jinx it by saying it aloud before I even knew what was going on. I needed time to think. I needed to be able to scrutinize and plan. I was a good planner and thinker, I told myself. I could figure out everything, but I just needed more time first. Then I would tell Rebecca, maybe.

"Mrs. Hart almost always gives a test on Mondays, but maybe she'll forgo her precious test this week. She missed it yesterday, but she sometimes skips a day to 'surprise' us on Tuesday instead," Rebecca replied. "I'm sure you have nothing to worry about," she continued. "You had all that time to study in the library."

She took a bite of the shortbread cookie she had been carrying. It was half gone and wouldn't last much longer, and I wondered if she was still on her first or already into her second. The shortbread cookies were as big around as large grapefruits. The few times I had bought a cookie from the student store, I had always gotten the snickerdoodles with cinnamon sugar on them, but I usually only ate half at a time and saved the other half for after lunch. I could understand Rebecca's obsession with the cookies every morning because in the morning, they were usually still hot, but she often treated herself to two on "special occasions." A special occasion for her might be a Friday before a weekend, the day after a test, the day of the test, the Tuesday after a three-day weekend, or a Monday or Wednesday. She had a lot of "special days," but I was okay with whatever. It wasn't like I was the food police or anything. Just because I noticed how many cookies she ate didn't mean I was in any way judging her. Her cookies were like my library. Everyone deserves to be comforted in whatever way that person chooses. Cookies and library books were far better than drugs or alcohol.

I kept quiet about what had gone on outside the library. I started thinking about Friday again and realized with apprehension that if I showed up at the game after telling her I wouldn't go, she might grow suspicious.

I took a breath to talk, but when I did, I remembered the clean soap scent mixed with flowers, leather, and that earthy-wood smell. I guess I held it because Rebecca looked at me and asked, "Elizabeth, are you okay? Do you have hiccoughs or something?"

"Yeah, no. I was just thinking I might go to the game after all on Friday."

"Really?" she asked, hope springing into her expression as she took another bite of her cookie. "We'll have so much fun…do you want to drive together…I usually sit by the pep band." She said all this in one rapid breath as if she were trying to get it all out before I changed my mind. As she talked, a few crumbs flew out of her mouth and one small chunk of her shortbread cookie actually came out of her mouth and fell on the ground. For a minute she looked down at it like she was considering picking it up.

"I'll probably drive by myself in case I decide to leave early or go to the dance or something, " I uttered as casually as I could manage.

"What?" she fired back in disbelief. "Have you ever even been to a dance?" she countercharged.

"I didn't say I was going to the dance. Just that I might go or do something else. Maybe I just want to try something new. I mean, there's more to life than just going to the library and studying, you know."

As I said it, I knew she didn't believe me. I didn't believe me. An aura of suspicion came over her face, and she stopped chewing, and she turned and stared at me, straight on. "Okay, what happened after you left me, and where is the real Elizabeth?"

I tried to laugh like she was joking, but as strange as Rebecca was, I couldn't be certain she wasn't serious. "Hey, it's my senior year. I figured I would give it a go. You're always pestering me to go to a game, and when I say I'll go, you start interrogating me. Do you want me to come or not?" One thing I knew about Rebecca was that she was a fairly passive person. She did not like confrontations. I felt bad for trying to use this knowledge to my advantage, but knowledge is meant to be used. I knew she would go along to get along.

She turned back to her cookie, which looked like it only had 2-3 bites left, finished the rest in one large bite, and then turned to me, trying to talk and not lose any more crumbs or pieces. "No, it sounds like fun. We'll have a blast."

I decided I might as well plunge ahead and have no surprises left to dread later. "Oh, and I want to sit on the northwest side of the stadium; that's the side that's closest to the locker rooms," I remarked.

"Wait, what? Why would you want to sit there? The pep band always sits in the upper tier near the northeast side," she argued.

"Look, maybe we can sit there part of the time and sit by the locker rooms part of the time," I said, trying to sound conciliatory. "I just think if I'm going to go to a football game, I should have the whole experience of watching the team come out onto the field and cheering them on throughout the game." I've read that every poker player has a tell. I wondered what mine was and if Rebecca could see it right now.

She thought for a moment. Her jaw worked a little as if she were still chewing on a cookie, even though I knew she had finished the last bite a couple of minutes before. "Okay," she said, "I guess that makes sense." I could tell she didn't really believe that. She was just happy to have someone to go with her so she wouldn't have to sit alone, which I knew she always did. "When do you think you'll get there?" she asked.

"What time does the game start?"

"Well, there's no JV game this week, so the varsity game starts at 7:30. It's usually about two hours long. I usually stay the whole time, but I've only been to a dance once. Honestly, they aren't very fun. The music is too loud and the concession stand only sells drinks, no food," she explained. "But the concession stand at the game sells lots of snacks: nachos, cokes, chips, hot dogs, soft pretzels…but no cookies, ice cream, or dessert-type food items." She sounded like she was writing a Yelp review.

"Okay, sounds good." I'll probably go around seven, then. I don't want to miss anything," I said.

"Wait a minute," she said. My chest felt like collywobbles suddenly gripped my lungs with the fear that she had figured out what was going on. I didn't even know why I was trying to keep it a secret. It wasn't like it was even a big deal or anything. I told myself that over and over, but I knew it wasn't true. Somehow, I had gone from not caring about football, or boys, or dances, or popularity to imagining a host of scenarios that were exciting and private. They were all decent and proper in my mind but very private since I had never really thought along those lines nor talked to anyone about boys before.

My mom had tried to give me The Talk when I turned 13 and both of us were so embarrassed by her attempt that we never broached the subject again. She had simply said that she was there for me when I was ready and that she wished she had a mom willing to talk when she had been my age.

My dad just said, "Stay away from boys until you're out of college. They're nothing but trouble, they're too immature, and they only want one thing." Luckily, he never explained what they wanted or how he knew that, but since he and my mom met in high school, I had a pretty idea I didn't want to find out. I tried not to even think about that.

"Do you want to go to GetaBurger or somewhere before the game? The food at the game is good for snacks, but I like to power up first, so I have a lot of energy for cheering," Rebecca explained.

I let out a breath I didn't know I had been holding. "Uh, I think I'll just eat something before I go," I said. "But thanks."

"Okay, but you have a few days to decide. If you change your mind, let me know."

"Sure thing," I said.

We switched topics abruptly and started talking about the possible science test. Rebecca had science during period 2, but I didn't have it until after lunch. We agreed to meet during lunch at the library--as we often did--and I would help her with her math homework, and she would tell me what I needed to study if there was a science test.

The periods seemed to roll by. In the first period, I read through my term paper about the women's suffrage movement. In the second period, I flew through my AP calculus homework so fast that I caught three mistakes when I went through them the second time. By the time lunch came around, I was relaxed, and the feeling of apprehension mixed with excitement had left me.

I made my way to the library after grabbing a strawberry Appleways bar and a bag of Cheez-Its from the student store. I ate the Appleways bar while walking through the Quad on my way to meet Rebecca. Every bite or two, I would look around to see if I could catch a glimpse of Blake, but I didn't see him. I realized it was interesting that I didn't remember ever seeing him in the Quad during lunch. He could go off campus during lunch since juniors and seniors could go off campus, or maybe I had just never really looked for him before.

By the time I got to the steps, I had finished my bar and was halfway into the bag of Cheez-Its. Rebecca was always a little later than I was because she went into the cafeteria and ate a hot lunch. I usually just went inside since she knew where I usually sat, but today, I decided to wait on the steps for her. After a few minutes, I saw her walking toward me. Her dark brown hair was now pulled back into a ponytail. She must have stuffed her Levi jacket in her backpack or locker because now she just had on a black tank top with some 80's metal band that I didn't recognize. Truth be told, I doubt she knew the band, either. She always picked clothes that she thought other kids would wear, but she was always a few decades behind. Her blue jeans had holes that were clearly cut with scissors to make near-perfect squares where her knees were. She looked like she was finishing up a cup of pudding or applesauce as she approached me.

"Hey, there's a lesson on forces and motion, but no test today," she said as soon as she was close enough.

I stood up from where I had been sitting on the marble steps and waited while she threw away her chocolate pudding cup. "Can you explain what the product rule is? Derivatives are so vile," she said.

"Hey, if you want my help, you won't badmouth calculus," I shot back. We headed up the steps and went into the near-empty library. Mrs. Young eyed us as we walked in as if we were shoplifters breaking and entering a store after hours.

"Hello, Mrs. Young," I greeted her as we were walking to the back table by the study rooms. The study rooms were for students to study and discuss things, but we usually just sat at one of the regular tables since there really wasn't anyone to disturb, and we were usually pretty quiet. The only other people in the library that we could see were a group of 3 boys in one of the study rooms playing chess and having some kind of semi-heated conversation. Two were seated and the one who was standing kept moving pieces and pointing. Although we couldn't hear them, the one who was standing must have been arguing about something.

We sat at a back table against the mint green wall that I suppose was meant to be a calming color. As we opened our textbooks and I pulled out my homework to show Rebecca how to work the equations, I finished off my bag of Cheez-Its which were covertly tucked in my backpack by my feet.

"You're such a rebel," joked Rebecca as I reached down and snuck one in my mouth. Mrs. Young was quite a distance away, sitting at her desk, but we were still within her field of vision, and she would look over at us every once in a while, peering at us through her horned-rimmed glasses as if she were on a stakeout looking for bank robbers.

We finished up pretty quickly as Rebecca rapidly caught on to how to do the problems. She's pretty smart. It's just that the teacher, Mr. Jennings, never explains things in a way that most kids would understand. He was a new teacher and fairly young but already was completely gray-haired. He would often start explaining a problem and would get off topic and end up talking about what he had for dinner the previous night or asking kids what they did over the weekend. Most kids loved him. He was an easy grader--I think because he felt guilty for being so easily distracted. Anytime a kid didn't understand a problem, the kid would ask an unrelated question, and Mr. Jennings would be off for the next 15 minutes before he remembered that he was supposed to be teaching math. Since I always looked ahead in the book, I usually understood what he was trying to teach before he even started the lesson.

We packed up our backpacks and headed out the door. On the way out, Mrs. Young called out, "Goodbye, Rebecca. Goodbye, Ann. Have a good rest of the day."

When we got outside, Rebecca turned to me and said in a low voice, "Isn't Ann your mom's name?"

"Yes," I replied. "That was kind of weird. She's never mixed me and my mom up before, and now she's done it for the second time today." We waited for the bell to ring in silence. I had science right after lunch, so we said goodbye, and I headed for the Quad. The science and economics building, Kennedy Center, was on the west side of the Quad, opposite the old Vocational buildings, which were east of the Quad but weren't in use anymore.

The Quad was still crowded with students finishing lunch or just sitting and talking, or even throwing a frisbee or football around. Blake wasn't there. I didn't wait outside but instead went right inside since the bell would ring in just a few minutes. I climbed the concrete stairs to the second floor, where Mrs. Hart's room was. Her door was open, so I went in and took my seat. She was writing a question on the board, "What are the five forces of motion?" without turning around, she said, "Good afternoon, Elizabeth. How are you today?"

I wasn't startled that she knew it was me. I was always the first one to class. "I'm okay, Mrs. Hart. How is your day going?"

"Periodically, I tend to be good," she replied with an attempt at humor. Mrs. Hart was always trying to introduce humor into her classroom and her lessons. She had a poster that said, "If a king farts, is it a noble gas?" Another handwritten poster said, "I've always had my ION you. You're just SODIUM cool. I can't find anything BORON about you. You're the mate for my SULFER ever!" She made class fun, and most kids liked her. When kids first saw her, the first thing they noticed about her was her height. 6'4" was very tall for any teacher, but she was easily the tallest female faculty member on campus. My guess is she got teased a lot when she was younger, so she developed a great sense of humor. She always wore a white lab coat even when we weren't doing lab work. It gave her the appearance of a doctor or bio-engineer. She had grayish brown hair that was cropped just below her ears, and her lab coat usually had a pair of safety goggles in the pocket.

The bell rang, and other students filtered in. Rebecca was right as usual, and we did not have a test, but I secretly was disappointed because I had already read the chapter on Newton's laws of motion and would have been ready for a test.

I went to the library after school and even lingered outside for several minutes before going in, but I did not see Blake. Perhaps he was at practice or with his friends. Either way, I had plenty to do because my term paper on the women's suffrage movement needed to be finished and annotated, and I wanted to be ahead in science and calculus, just in case.

Thursday was pretty much the same, and I started thinking that maybe I had overthought the whole situation with Blake. Maybe he just wanted more fans at the game and I had imagined any interest he had in hanging out with me. Except he had specifically mentioned going out afterward to the dance or to talk. I was confused, but then I was in uncharted territory. Normally, I have every aspect of my day, week, life…planned out. There are no surprises. I think of every scenario and plan for every contingency. I typically detest surprises, but I had to admit that this Friday was a surprise I was looking forward to. It was fun trying to figure out what it all meant. However, I had no clue why Blake would even want to hang out with me when he could go out with any girl on campus. In the back of my mind, I allowed a small spot of hope to grow.

He likes that you're smart, I told myself. He said I was the only person who understood him, but I really didn't know him. Was he really that alone? His mom had left him and it sounded like he tried to avoid his dad as much as possible. It sounded like people only talked to him about football. I wondered if the ball he carried around with him all the time was part of his mask. He seemed to cover up the real person and hide a lot from people--except, for a brief moment, he had opened up to me. I was sure he didn't go around telling people they didn't know the real Blake that he felt invisible. So why had he told me, I wondered. My mind went over everything again and again like a complicated calculus equation that I couldn't seem to solve, no matter how many times I went over the details. I knew there were more variables that I just didn't know, more information that would make everything balance and make sense. For now, there was nothing to do but wait and see.

CHAPTER 2
I'M NOT THAT NERVOUS

Friday morning, I woke up early, even for me. It was 5:15, but I told myself I wanted to review the chapter we covered this week in calculus--even though I knew the real reason was because this was probably the last chance to see Blake before the game tonight. I would probably not go to the library after school since I would have to go home and get ready for the night's festivities, and Blake would probably do whatever it was that football players did before a game. I went down for breakfast, deciding on eggs since a lot of teachers give tests on Fridays, and I wanted something low in sugar.

I was just finishing my eggs when my mom came down the stairs and into the kitchen. She was dressed in tan slacks a cream-colored blouse with small green polka dots on it, but she still had on house slippers. "You're up earlier than usual," she said, trying to hide a yawn as she spoke.

"Yeah, I just wanted to get an early start," I said. She looked at me like she knew there was something more going on but didn't say anything. I swallowed another bite of eggs and said, "Hey, Mom. I thought I might go to the game tonight."

"The football game?" she asked. Her eyebrows were raised up in disbelief.

"Of course, the football game," I replied. "Rebecca goes every week, and she talked me into it." It was just a little fib, I told myself. "She says they're really fun."

"Is that the weird girl who believes in vampires and UFOs?" she asked.

"Mom, I wish you wouldn't call my friends weird," I replied. "But yeah, that's her," I admitted. I walked over to the sink, rinsed my plate, and put it in the dishwasher. "She's not that weird once you get to know her," I said defensively.

"If you say so," she replied. "So, are you meeting anyone else there tonight?" she inquired. She had a slight grin like she knew there was more going on. Maybe she was just glad to see me going out, I told myself.

"I don't know," I replied. Now, I knew it was more than a little fib. "I might hang out afterward or go to the dance."

"The dance?" she practically yelled. "Who are you, and what have you done with my daughter?" she joked. Now, she was practically beaming.

"I don't know," I continued. "Maybe I'll just come home afterward." I just don't want you to be worried if I stay out a little later."

"Stay out as late as you want," she replied a little too quickly. "Call us if you need a ride home."

"Why would I need a ride home," I asked. "I have my Civic."

"Well, if you don't think it's safe for you to drive for any reason, just call us. That's all I'm saying," she explained.

It was getting a little awkward, so I said goodbye and left. My mom always seemed to be able to sense things and read my mind when something was wrong. When I got to school, I decided to walk by the library on the way to the student store just in case Blake was there. This would mean I would have to go a long way around, past the vocational ed buildings, and come from the northeast and walk across the street to the northwest. I was earlier than normal, so I would still have plenty of time to meet Rebecca at the student store and then head back to the library for a second chance at seeing Blake.

I got all the way to the library steps and lingered just in case, but nobody popped up to take my books today.

Not even one of Rebecca's vampires. I hung around as long as I could without feeling like an oddball and started walking south back to the Quad. The grass was wet with dew and cool this early in the morning. The maintenance mows the Quad on Thursdays after school so it still had a freshly mowed smell. I passed the science/econ Kennedy Center on my right, and in just a few minutes, I was at the student store. Rebecca was already there in line, the only person waiting for it to open.

"Hi, Elizabeth. Ready for the game tonight?" she asked. I could tell she was excited and I think she was afraid I would back out. She was wearing white jean shorts today and a black shirt with our school logo on it that said *Wildcat Pride*. "Sure," I said. "We'll meet at six on the northwest side of the stadium where the players come out from the locker room."

"I can't wait," she replied. Her enthusiasm changed her whole expression. Usually Rebecca is always very energetic, but this was probably the happiest I had seen her since she made the debate team her freshman year. She was talking about how much fun we would have and asking me if I was sure I didn't want to go to Getaburger to eat first when she just froze mid-sentence. Her eyes were big and looking behind me.

I turned around to see what she was staring at, and as I turned, I heard Blake's deep, staccato voice call out, "Hey, Beth. You're here early. Hey, Becca--wait, do you go by Becca, Rebecca, or Reb?" Blake asked. Blake was dressed the same as I had always seen him: faded jeans, a clean black T-shirt, and checkered Vans. He had his letterman jacket on with the big R for Ridgeview and a picture of a wildcat on it. In his right hand was the old football he always carried around. He was too far away for me to smell his clean soap smell with a hint of leather and cedar wood, but I still imagined I smelled it.

Rebecca was too mesmerized to answer.

"Um, yeah," I stumbled out a reply. "We come here early on Fridays to study for any tests that might come up on Fridays. And she probably doesn't care what you call her, right, Rebecca? Rebecca still just stared with her mouth wide open. "You're pretty early, yourself," I said.

"Yeah, I come early on Fridays to go walk around on the field, get my mind focused on the game, or just clear my head. I like how peaceful it is in the mornings. Nobody yelling, nothing but quiet," he explained. After a pause, he asked, "Are we still on for tonight?"

"Uh, yeah," I stammered. "I'll be on the northwest side, by the lockers, right?"

"Don't forget to wait for me after the game. I'll come get you."

"I won't forget," I promised--thinking I couldn't forget if I fell and suffered a serious concussion. It was all I could think about.

"Okay then. See you tonight," he said and walked away before I could respond.

I looked over at Rebecca, and her mouth was still open. Her eyes followed him until he walked around the corner and out of sight. She seemed to snap out of her paralysis and slugged me in the upper arm. "What was that about?" She demanded. "You know Blake Patterson? What's going on here?" she fired off in rapid succession.

"I just met him recently. He seems nice, so we're going to hang out after the game," I replied as nonchalantly as I could.

"How does he know who I am? Did you tell him about me?"

"I don't know how he knows your name," I answered. "I didn't talk about you. I don't even know how he knew my name."

"Elizabeth, you expect me to believe that?" she demanded. "Everybody at school probably knows you. You're the smartest person here--and that includes the teachers--but I'm a nobody." I had no answer to that, and as we waited for the student store to open, Rebecca made me go over the details of what had happened. I kept the details sparse since I didn't really know myself why Blake had asked me out or what--if anything--was happening.

I was grateful to finally have someone to talk to about Blake. In the end, Rebecca was just as baffled as I was, but she still talked about it as if she didn't completely believe me, as if I was holding something back that would explain everything.

When the student store opened, I was surprised to see that Rebecca only bought one cookie. I had been sure she would deem this a "special occasion" that required two cookies, but she said the news about Blake would sustain her as if she had eaten a dozen cookies. We went to the library but didn't really study much. I think we both left for the first period in very high spirits.

The day flew by, and I don't even remember the tests I took, but I knew the material and was sure I had done well, even if I couldn't remember much afterward. I went straight home after school. I changed three times before settling on a dark blue blouse that had frilly sleeves that came down almost to my elbows. I decided on blue jeans rather than a skirt since I didn't know if we would be going to the dance or somewhere else. I thought about putting my hair in a ponytail but decided it made me look too young.

About this time, my mom came and stood in the doorway. "You look very nice, sweety," she said. "If you want to borrow any make-up or jewelry, let me know."

"Do you think I need makeup?" I asked. The thought hadn't even occurred to me. I never wore makeup, but I knew most girls did.

"Not at all," my mom replied. "You're naturally beautiful. Whatever makes you comfortable."

Yeah, comfortable…like that was going to happen. I couldn't decide if I should eat dinner or grab a snack at the game. I couldn't even remember what I had eaten for lunch. I decided I was too nervous to eat anything right then, so I skipped dinner and finished getting ready. By the time I was finished, it was after 5. Dad came in the house just as I was getting ready to leave, and I was glad I wouldn't have to spend too much time talking to him about tonight or getting an awkward speech about being "careful." My parents are too open about certain subjects sometimes, and I'm usually more uncomfortable than they are discussing personal issues.

Dad set down his briefcase by the door when he saw me and gave me a hug. "What are you all dressed up for?" he asked.

"Nothing," I replied. "Just going to the football game tonight."

"Going to the football game?" he repeated like he hadn't heard me correctly.

"David, she's just going to the game to hang out with some friends. I'll tell you about it later during dinner," my mom answered. She and my dad shared a kind of knowing look, like they were sharing some secret information or something.

"Well, have fun, Elizabeth," he said. "Don't forget you can always call us if you need a ride home."

I sighed heavily. "Yes, mom told me that."

"I told her that, dear," my mom said at the same time.

I headed out the door, and it wasn't long before I was in my blue Honda Civic, headed to unchartered territory. My first game. I was glad I hadn't eaten anything because I was so nervous. I doubt I would have been able to keep anything down. When I used to ride the bus, it took over an hour to get to school, even though our house was only about 15-20 minutes away.

When I got to school, I pulled around to the north parking lot by the stadium. The stadium had a separate parking lot and entrance just past the staff parking lot. It was barely 6 o'clock, but the parking lot was already half full. Once the lot filled up, there was another dirt parking lot behind it where people could still park, but it was a dirt lot with no pavement. Next to the main stadium entrance, there was a separate entrance door where athletes could enter and go straight into the locker room. Although there was a girls' and boys' locker room, only the boys had a separate entrance. Any girls' teams would have to enter through the main entrance and enter their locker room from the front side, inside the stadium. There were some pick-up trucks next to the outside boys' entrance, and I wondered if one of them was Blake's or if he drove something else.

I had told Rebecca that I would meet her inside, but she was waiting by the ticket booth to the left of the main entrance. She waved excitedly as I walked toward the entrance. She had on a Ridgeview Wildcat school shirt that she had probably just bought at the student store earlier that day. She also had changed out her jean shorts for white jeans, and she had on the black boots that added an inch or two to her height, making her possibly 5'2" if she stretched her neck up. Her dark, curly hair was pulled back in a ponytail tied back with a purple and gold ribbon--our school colors. Knowing her, I was surprised she didn't sport a RWC in gold and purple paint on her face. I was never sure whether she had an abnormally high amount of school spirit or if she did everything just to try to fit in.

I walked up to her, and her smile practically blinded me. I didn't remember ever seeing her so happy. "Hey, Elizabeth. This is going to be so much fun. You'll be so glad you came," she said with a bit too much enthusiasm.

"Sounds like it'll be a blast," I answered back, trying to sound just as eager.

"Don't be nervous," she said. "It's just a game. Plus, we're favored to win."

Clearly, I was more nervous than I thought if Rebecca could tell. Usually she had a difficult time picking up social cues or other's emotions. She had misread the reason why I was nervous, but the fact that she could sense it at all meant I must be broadcasting it like a radio tower. I took a few silent, deep breaths and started thinking about the doubling sequence in my head. I would sometimes do the doubling sequence where I start with 1, then 2, then 4, and 8, and so on, doubling each number until the number got high enough to distract me. I usually get at least 20 numbers, but I've been able to get 30 numbers before. Tonight, I only got to 32768 before I was having to concentrate hard on what was next. It's difficult to concentrate when you have a friend staring at you with undisguised anticipation.

"I'm not nervous," I lied. I've just never been to a game and don't know what to expect.

"That's what I'm here for," replied Rebecca. Right then, I was so glad she was there, but I felt guilty that I would be leaving her after the game to go to the dance or talk or whatever it was I was going to do with Blake. Rebecca seemed to read my mind. "Don't worry. After the game, I'm going home, and you and your football star date will be all alone," she teased. "But if you don't mind, maybe you can watch me until I get to my car to make sure I make it out safely."

"Rebecca, vampires are not going to get you on your way to your car," I said. I smiled, and my nervousness eased as I got a mental picture of Rebecca running to her car while being chased by bats.

We waited in line, got our tickets, and went through the gate and through the concrete tunnel that goes under the concrete stadium seats, splitting the boys' lockers from the girls'. We were on the Home side, so we had concrete bleachers stretching east and west along the north side of the stadium. Underneath the concrete bleachers were the locker rooms on the far end. Across the field were the metal, collapsible bleachers for the visiting side. The pep band was already sitting to our left as we exited the tunnel. They sat in the upper section of the bleachers on the east side of the stadium. Rebecca waved at them as we turned and headed in the opposite direction, but I didn't see anyone wave back. We walked along the lower section in front of the concrete bleachers to the northwest side of the stadium, where the door to the locker room was.

The stadium was probably about a third full, but our section was nearly empty. When we got to our seats, Rebecca reached into a bag that she had been carrying and pulled out a little one-inch foam pad. It was purple and had the emblem of a Wildcat on it, but unlike her shirt, it looked like it was well used. "These seats are so hard," she explained. "Sorry, I didn't have time to get you one."

"That's okay," I said. I looked around at other people sitting in the stands but didn't see anyone else with a chair pad. We were at the 20-yard line, sitting about four rows back. Most of the people were to the left of us, closer to where we came in at the 50-yard line. The pep band was about as far from us as possible without moving to the visitor's side of the field. We waited about 5 minutes, and Rebecca said, "I'm going to the concession stand before the line gets too long. Do you want anything?"

I hadn't eaten dinner yet, but I wasn't really hungry, so I declined, and when she left, I looked around again. I couldn't see the door to the locker room, but I knew it was nearly straight in front of where I was sitting. To the left, around the 50-yard line, there was a long metal bench set back away from the field about five feet in front of the concrete stadium bleachers. About 20 yards past, that was a string of purple and yellow balloons strung together where I supposed the cheerleaders would be. The pep band was warming up with the song "Go, Fight, Win."

After a few minutes, Rebecca came back carrying a tray of nachos, a bag of sour cream and onion chips, two hot dogs, a soft pretzel, and a Coke. I marveled that she was able to carry it all without dropping anything and said jokingly, "Well, if you don't end up as a veterinarian, you'd make a great waitress." She had said since 6th grade that she wanted to be a veterinarian, but not a normal veterinarian. She had some ideas about studying bats and finding a "cure" for vampirism. I often wondered how much she told me was serious and how much she was pulling my leg.

"Mmmh," she replied after stuffing half a hot dog in her mouth. She chattered between bites about the game stats and different players. I was surprised that she actually seemed to know a lot about our team. I knew next to nothing except that we were supposed to be pretty good and that Blake was thought of as one of the best quarterbacks who had played for our school in several years. Because of that, our stadium was filling up with students and parents alike. School spirit abounded.

Rebecca had finished her hot dogs and nachos. She put the soft pretzel and chips in her bag and pulled out something wrapped in a napkin. She set it on her lap and took a sip of coke. Then she unwrapped the napkin and revealed a shortbread cookie. She must have gone back to the store earlier today at school since I knew she had only bought one cookie this morning.

She saw me looking at her cookie and reluctantly asked, "Want half?"

I was taken aback that she would offer. She must really be glad I had come. "No, thanks," I replied. I could tell she was relieved as she took another bite. We continued to talk as we waited for the game to start. She mostly did the talking, and I mostly did the listening, but that was okay.

The pep band started playing "We Will Rock You," and the cheerleaders came over in front of us with a big paper banner that said Ridgeview Wildcats on it. The team came out and tore through the sign. I couldn't tell which player was Blake, but Rebecca must have figured out what I was searching for because she yelled in my ear, "Blake is number 16 there in the front."

I saw number 16 at the front with his purple and gold helmet on. His jersey had the number 16 and the name Patterson on it. The other players ran across the field and then came back to stand in front of the coach, but Blake went to the 50-yard line in the center of the field, where a referee was with the quarterback from the other team. The referee threw a coin in the air and let it land on the grass. He picked it up and showed it to both players. Blake pointed downfield, and Rebecca said, "We get the ball first."

Blake came back to the sideline where the coach and other players were, and some of the other players went out onto the field. The opposing team lined up and kicked the ball. A player on our side waved his hand and, caught the ball around the 10-yard line, and then ran with the ball. He avoided a couple of tackles but was brought down near the 30-yard line. Blake came back out with some other players and lined up. The play started, and Blake acted like he gave the ball to someone else, then stepped back and threw the ball downfield, where another player from our team caught it and ran until he was tackled near the 15-yard line.

"Wow," exclaimed Rebecca. We're already within scoring distance." I wasn't sure exactly what that meant, but I had an idea that Blake had made a pretty good play. On the next play, Blake again pretended to hand the ball to someone, but this time, he kept the ball and ran with it around other players all the way into the end zone. The crowd screamed wildly, and Rebecca joined them and yelled, "Touchdown!" I was caught up in the excitement as well. Even though I didn't really understand the game, I could tell we had scored and that Blake was very good.

The team lined up again and kicked the ball through the goalposts. The rest of the game was just as exciting-- probably more so for our team than for the opposing team since they fell further and further behind. Every so often, the pep band would play some song, and the crowd would cheer and yell. I had to admit that even if I hadn't met Blake, I still was having a lot of fun.

It was just after 9 when the game ended, with our team scoring 49 and the other team scoring 13. I knew with the game being over that soon I would be alone with Blake for whatever he had planned, but I was strangely relaxed. The crowd was filtering out, and soon, very few were left in the stands.

Rebecca turned and said, "Well, I better get to my car while there's still people around…unless you want to walk me there. I mean, you could walk me there quickly and then come right back." She sounded desperate, and even though I knew it was all in her head, I felt guilty saying no.

"I don't want Blake to come out and see me not here and think I changed my mind and left," I explained.

"Of course. That makes sense," replied Rebecca with a long sigh. "I hadn't thought about that. I'll be fine," she said. Her voice sounded a little shaky. She probably was used to walking out with the pep band surrounding her or at least a lot of people, and even though I knew there weren't vampires, gargoyles, or other creatures waiting to swoop down on her, I did feel responsible.

"I'll try to check on you on the way out. I'll look for your car. I know what it looks like. If it's gone, then I know you got out okay." She cheered up a little.

"Yeah, thanks. That would be nice of you."

So she walked down the steps and through the tunnel which led to the parking lot and soon I was nearly alone. There were still a few people hanging out--parents or friends of football players. I was alone in my section of the bleachers. The bright stadium lights were still on and a few bats were flying around catching bugs around the field. I thought of Rebecca and what she would say if she saw the bats. I smiled and was thinking about her when Blake stepped up beside me. I hadn't even seen him come out of the locker rooms.

His dark, curly hair was damp but I couldn't tell if it was from showering or from sweating during the game. He had on his leatherman's jacket over his black T-shirt and was back to wearing his faded jeans and checkered vans.

"Hey, Beth. Glad you could stick around," he said. He smiled his crooked smile, and I couldn't help but smile back.

I wasn't sure what to say and said the first thing that popped into my head. "You were so good during the game." I immediately wished I hadn't said it. Blake looked a little embarrassed. Surely he was used to compliments about his playing. Maybe people only saw him as a football player, and as he said, he felt invisible at times. Maybe that's what he had meant. My mind raced to think of something non-football related to talk about. "Do you mind if we walk to the parking lot really quickly?" I asked. I just want to make sure my friend, Rebecca, made it to her car okay."

"She's the one who believes in vampires, right?" he asked in an amused tone.

"Yeah, but how did you know that," I asked.

"Pretty much everyone at school knows that," he replied with his big crooked smile to show what he thought of it. "But it's okay. Everyone has to believe in something."

"That's very understanding of you," I replied. Inside, I kicked myself. That was the response an overly polite grandmother would say, not a senior in high school on a date.

We walked down the steps and through the tunnel to the parking lot. The bottom of the tunnel was dirt, but it wasn't muddy. I wondered why the school had never paved it over. There were pieces of chewing gum stuck along the wall as Blake, and I walked the 20 or so steps to the parking lot, and I wondered what we would be doing after this. Would we go to the dance, to GetaBurger, walk around, or something else? We exited the tunnel and stepped onto the asphalt parking lot. Rebecca's car was still there, but I didn't see Rebecca by it.

I glanced around and saw her off to the left. There were three boys by her. I couldn't hear what they were saying, but she looked very uncomfortable and petrified. Blake started walking faster, straight to them.

Rebecca had her back against a car, and the three boys were in a semi-circle around her. As we got closer, I could hear some of what they were saying, and after a few seconds, I became so angry that I forgot they were much bigger than I was. I quickened my pace, but Blake got there before I did. They turned as he approached and the close one sneered at Blake as Blake came up to him.

The boy on the left wore dark jeans that looked a few sizes too big to fit him, black boots, and a red plaid, long-sleeve shirt untucked. His dark hair was cropped close to his head. He was much shorter and slimmer than Blake or than the other two. The boy in the middle was easily the largest one. He was taller than Blake, who I knew was almost as tall as Mrs. Hart, so this boy must have been at least 6'5". He looked like he weighed a lot more than Blake, but unlike Blake, his weight covered him in a soft, doughy way that, had he been shorter, would have made him look obese rather than intimidating. The top of his reddish-blond hair was pulled into a ponytail, and the sides and back were buzzed short. He had on a dark blue T-shirt and khaki pants that were also baggy with no belt and dirty white tennis shoes. He was smoking but held the cigarette between his thumb and forefinger close to Rebecca's face, clearly threatening her with it by bringing it close to her face as he talked. The boy on the right looked like he could have been the middle boy's brother. He was a couple of inches shorter but had the same reddish-blond hair. He also had a reddish-brown goatee. A thick gold chain hung over his shirt--which was also a Ridgecrest Wildcats school shirt. He was nearly the same height as Blake but thinner. A Lot of his height looked like it came from his neck, which, for some reason, looked extra long, as if it had grown stretched out. Each boy was a couple of feet apart, with enough space between them to see Rebecca but not enough room for her to get by them.

As Blake approached them, instead of stopping a couple of feet away as they expected, he turned, dipped down a little, and drove his shoulder into the solar plex of the middle boy, driving him back into the car. Rebecca moved away to her right as the boy was slammed into the car. He bent over, trying to catch his breath, but before he even straightened up, Blake stepped to the right and shoved the boy, who looked like his brother, back with both hands. The boy stumbled back and almost fell but caught himself about four feet back. Now, there was one boy close to us on the left, the middle boy who was still bent over, and the boy on the right who was back a few feet. Rebecca stood with her back against the car a couple of feet away from the boy who was bent over.

"What's up with you? We were just talking. You think that just because you're a star on the field, that means anything here? This doesn't involve you," said the boy on the left.

"You need to leave," was all Blake said in reply. A heavy silence surrounded him. He had a calm, prepared look in his eyes, like a predatory animal standing guard over a kill, ready to kill to protect it. The boy on the left stared at Blake with open hatred expressed on his features. The boy on the right looked ready to charge back in. I was shaking with adrenaline, but Blake stood calmly in place. He seemed composed, as if waiting for another football play to begin on the field. Blake looked back and forth among the three, looking each one in the eyes. His expression was unreadable but confident.

Finally, without saying anything, the boy in the middle straightened up and stormed off. The other two followed without a word. The shorter boy, who had been on the left, looked back over his shoulder as he walked away. His face bore disdain and contempt.

I half walked--half ran to Rebecca. She was shaking and looked short and pale, and I could tell she was shaking, although she tried to hide it. "Are you okay?" I asked.

She tried to answer, but she seemed incapable of speech. After a minute, she drew a shaky breath and whispered, "I'm okay." Even that seemed like it took a lot of effort for her to utter.

Blake stepped up, taking off his letterman's jacket. He draped it around her shoulders. "Do you feel up to walking to your car, Becca?" he asked.

At once, Rebecca seemed to regain her senses. "Oh yeah," she said. I'm fine. Thanks for the assist." She stood up a little straighter.

Blake smiled his half-crooked smile. "Luckily, they were only humans and not creatures of the night," he said.

I almost laughed. He said it in a way that was reassuring rather than derisive. This seemed to bolster Rebecca even further and she seemed to regain the rest of her composure.

Rebecca smiled and replied, "I'm sure you could have handled them either way." I looked over at her and although I tried to hide it, a slight smile crept to the corners of my lips. I looked over at Rebecca. Even under the parking lot lights, I could tell she was blushing.

Blake put his arm around her shoulder and started walking toward her car. There were only a few cars in the parking lot left. Blake guided her to the north, where the few remaining cars were parked. Rebecca already had her keys out and veered slightly to her right to her car, which was not much farther from where she had been standing. She drove a black Audi TTS that would look out of place in the teachers' parking lot, let alone the students.

When we got to her car, she used her remote and unlocked the doors. She still had on Blake's leatherman jacket, which hung down to her knees and started taking it off when Blake put his hand on her shoulder and stopped her.

"You can keep that and give it back to Beth tomorrow, and I can get it from her on Monday," Blake offered.

Now Rebecca's smile radiated. "Wow, you're so gallant," she said. I looked over at Blake, slightly embarrassed, but he seemed unaffected by her nerdiness. Blake leaned over and opened the door. Rebecca seemed completely recovered as she slid into the driver's seat. She looked up at us through the open door as she started the Audi TTS. "You two, be careful. There's a full moon tonight."

"Blake managed a serious look on his face as he replied, "Don't worry. I won't let any of the undead or unholy creatures hurt Beth."

Rebecca shut the door and drove off. I saw her watching us off and on in her rearview mirror until the car turned onto the street.

Now, it was just Blake and me. We were alone. I didn't know what we would be doing or where we would be going, but I decided I trusted him and that it wouldn't matter where we went or what we did. As the first dates went, this had already set records. Of course, I had nothing to compare it to since this was literally my first date ever, but I figured Blake was probably used to dating, and I pushed that thought to the back of my mind.

"I don't really have any plans," Blake said, breaking the silence. "I know where there's a party going on, but I try to stay away from those. I stop in but never stay long. Everyone is always drunk, and sometimes they get out of hand. If I wanted that, I'd just stay home with my dad. He drinks a lot. By a lot, I mean all the time."

Now, I felt a little awkward. Blake sounded like his home life was pretty bad with his mom leaving him and his dad drinking a lot." Inwardly, I felt guilty because my home was so different. The biggest problem I had at home in the last year was trying to convince my parents to let me get contacts. I realized that I hadn't said anything, and the awkward silence was becoming even more awkward. "I'm sorry," I said. "That sounds rough."

"Sorry, I don't know why I'm dumping this on you like this," he explained. "I usually keep everything inside and have a hard time talking to anyone. Somehow, I just feel like I can talk to you. Like you won't judge me. Like you don't expect me to be perfect, or just a quarterback, or...I don't know. This probably isn't making sense. We just met."

"No, it's okay," I offered. "I don't mind. I mean, you can talk to me about anything. Don't feel pressured one way or another. We can walk around and talk. To be honest, I didn't know what to expect tonight, but so far, I'm enjoying it." I cringed inwardly as I said this. I felt like I was being a complete dweeb. Blake had opened up to me, and that was all I could come up with in response.

"Anyway," I pressed on because when there's silence, I tend to want to fill it, "thanks for what you did for Rebecca. That was scary. Do you know those guys?"

"I used to," he said. The two big ones are Joey and Kenny MacGruber. Joey used to be on the football team my first two years, but then he graduated. His brother Kenny was on the team, but he got kicked off for drugs. They still come to some of the games, but they're punks. They like to intimidate people, but they back down when they're really challenged. That's why I came at them like that. I knew they would back down."

"What would have happened if they hadn't backed down?" I asked. "Or to Rebecca if we hadn't been there?" Both possibilities scared me.

"I don't think they would have really hurt Becca. They were more getting their kicks out of scaring her, but to be honest, they've changed since I knew them, so it was probably a good thing we were here just in case. If nothing else, they wouldn't have hurt her with witnesses around."

I noticed he hadn't answered what he would have done if they hadn't backed down, but maybe it was better if I didn't know. "So, what do you usually do after a game?" I asked to change the subject.

"Sometimes I go to an after-game party, but they're pretty boring. Everyone gets drunk, and all they want to talk about is the football game. I mean, I like football, but that's not all there is," he said. "Sometimes I feel like football is a trap, and other times I feel like it's my only escape. A lot of times, I just walk around and clear my head… thinking about my mom, my life, and things like that. I spend a lot of time alone, and usually, it doesn't bother me, but lately, I feel like I need to reach out to someone, or I'll drown."

I didn't know what to say to that. His life was so different from mine. I had everything planned out. I took my parents for granted. I hadn't experienced anything like what Blake was living and going through. Usually, I always had an answer to everything; I usually thought I knew everything. Here I was out of my depth in something I had no clue about. I felt like I had to say something. Blake sounded so downhearted. "It sounds like you have it pretty difficult," I said. "Has it always been like that?"

"It was different before my mom left," he explained. I knew she was unhappy, but I had no idea how much until she was gone."

"Well, maybe she'll come back, and you can go be with her again someday," I offered, not knowing what else to say.

He had an odd expression on his face like he was looking far away into the future. "Maybe someday," he replied.

"Anyway, you sound very smart, and I know you said people only think of you as a football player, but I can tell you're definitely much more," I said.

His crooked smile lit up his face, and I could tell it was genuine this time, not a mask like in front of the library. "I'm good at reading people, but I'm not book-smart like you," he responded.

We talked as we walked along aimlessly. We walked south toward the Quad. The grass was slightly damp and clung to my shoes as we walked beneath the tall elm trees. A light breeze played with my hair. I relaxed and started talking about school, classes, grades, my family, college…After a while, I realized that Blake had been quiet the whole time I had been talking. Blake was very polite and had listened to me rattle on, but I didn't know if he was really interested in school or college. I felt guilty for monopolizing the conversation. I had a sense that Blake had asked me out because he needed someone to listen to him, not to prattle on about trivial things. "You must think I'm very self-centered talking about myself so much," I mentioned. "So, what are your plans? I mean, after high school," I asked him.

He stopped walking, and his eyebrows drew down as if he was thinking about it seriously for the first time. "I don't really have any plans," he finally answered. He walked over to a concrete and rock bench that surrounded a tall elm tree and acted as both a bench and a planter. We sat on the cold stone, slightly facing each other, our knees touching. He didn't explain, and I fought the urge to jump in and start talking again. I could tell he was still thinking about it. Finally, he broke the silence. "To be honest, I just try to get by day to day. I mean, I'd like to go to college and play football, but all I really want to do is get out of my house and maybe meet someone I can talk to. I mean, really talk." He looked at me when he said this. My chest felt hot but I shivered with cold when he said this. The moon made his shiny, dark curls stand out.

I felt my cheeks grow warm against the cool night air and could imagine them darkening to a deep, rosy red as I involuntarily blushed. I wondered if I was imagining his words carrying a deeper meaning than he intended. We barely met, I told myself. Still, I felt more comfortable and relaxed than I usually did around anyone, even my parents. With Rebecca or the few other friends I had, I usually only talked about grades, classes, and superficial things. With Blake, I felt like I could tell him anything.

"Do you ever feel alone and trapped?" he suddenly asked.

Caught off guard, I didn't know what to say. "Honestly, I feel pretty lucky compared to a lot of people, but sometimes I do feel like people only see me as a bookworm, a kind of a walking, living, breathing encyclopedia," I said it before I really thought about it, but after it was out, I realized it was true.

"That's exactly how I feel," said Blake. People see me and only see a dumb jock quarterback."

"And you don't have anyone to talk to?" I asked.

"The guys on the team don't care about anything but partying and getting with as many girls as possible," he said. He looked down, a little embarrassed. "I mean, nobody knows about my dad or mom. I've never told anyone. Except for you now. And nobody ever asked because nobody cares. All they care about is how I throw a football." He held up the football as he said this as if to emphasize the point.

"You don't think carrying around a football everywhere underscores that point?" I asked.

"Yeah, but even without it people just thought of me as the quarterback of the school. I made quarterback my freshman year. That's not very common. My mom used to come to my games, and she gave me this football when she was still around. It was probably the last thing she gave me before leaving. I guess I just have a hard time letting go of it."

"I guess that makes sense," I said. "But why haven't you told anyone else? I'm sure everyone would understand."

"Sorry, but you're wrong there. People only care about themselves. You're special, so you don't see it. You care about others, and that's rare. Normal people aren't like that. Everyone else is all about, 'How does everything affect me?'"

"Did you just say I'm not normal?" I joked, trying to lighten the mood.

"Well, you're not. I don't really know you that well, but like I said, I can read people really well, and you are special. I know a lot of people at this school, and they all seem so shallow, but you're not shallow. You're unusual. You're more of an individual because you do what you want, and you don't seem to care what people think. That's rare, Beth."

I didn't know what to say. I didn't really think of myself much in terms of self-examination. It was true that I didn't seem to fit in all the time and didn't care, but lots of people didn't fit in. Like Rebecca not fitting in--except that she was always trying to fit in, be like everyone else. Maybe he was right. Without even knowing me for long, he had somehow gained some secret knowledge, some personal enlightenment about me that I didn't even know about myself.

"Well, I can tell that you're definitely special too, certainly more than just a football player. You really see people. That's a gift."

Blake smiled broadly. His teeth were straight and white, but I liked how one side of his mouth was higher than the other side, giving him a crooked smile that seemed almost mischievous. His smile matched his ice-blue eyes that seemed even paler because his skin was deeply tanned and his curly hair was so dark.   We sat in comfortable silence, our knees touching each other.

Even though I knew we had just met, I felt strangely comfortable with Blake, like I could ask him anything. "Can I ask you something?" I said, interrupting the silence. I didn't wait for an answer. "What was your mom like?" I knew it was a risky question, but Blake seemed so perceptive that I couldn't imagine him picking that up from his dad. I didn't know much of anything about either of his parents, but it sounded like his dad was always drinking and angry. I figured Blake had to have gotten his personality from his mom.

He brooded for a couple of minutes and I started to think I had overstepped the imaginary line somehow, but then he looked up and answered. "My mom was very warm and understanding, but I didn't know her as well as I had thought. I can usually read people and know their emotions and figure out what they're thinking, but my mom kept everything bottled up inside. I didn't know how isolated she must have felt until it was too late. Now I know exactly how she felt."

"I'm sorry," I apologized. "We don't have to talk about it."

"No, it's okay. One of the things I like about you is that you're direct. You say what you are thinking. A lot of people just say what they think I want to hear. It's boring being around people who always just tell you how great you are."

"Oh yea, I hate people always telling me how great I am," I joked. I laughed a little and Blake joined in.

"Seriously, I know you're kidding, but you don't even know how smart and beautiful you are," he said.

I could feel myself blushing again. Blake thought I was beautiful? I hoped he couldn't read me right then, but suddenly he smiled an enormous smile and I knew he could tell exactly what I was thinking.

"I'm really enjoying tonight, Beth, more than you know," he uttered.

"Yeah, me too," I replied feeling that I probably didn't need to say anything because it was obvious how I felt.

"It's nearly 11," he explained. "What time do you need to get back?"

It couldn't possibly be that late I thought. I checked my phone and wondered how Blake knew the time when he hadn't even checked. I had no curfew, but my mom had said before that if I was after midnight, I needed to call or text to let them know I was okay. It was sort of a curfew without being a real curfew. I had never come close to being out past midnight so they never felt the need to impose harsh restrictions. Still, I knew tonight couldn't last forever, however much I wanted it to. "I guess I should get back," I said.

We stood up and started walking back across the grass of the Quad to the parking lot in front of the stadium.

As we walked Blake reached over and grabbed my hand. My pulse quickened and I wondered if Blake would be able to feel my heartbeat pounding through my hand. His hand was soft, but firm. I could feel calluses on the fingertips and upper palm. Even without a jacket, his hand was warm though I could see goosebumps on his forearms and biceps. I tried to walk slowly, to savor every minute, but soon we were stepping onto the asphalt of the parking lot. The yellow-orange lights were still on and cast a dim glow on the single car left--my blue Honda Civic.

"Where's your car?" I asked, looking around.

"We only have one truck and my dad uses it for work so I walk most days," he explained. "He lets me use it when I really need it," he added.

"Do you need a ride?" I asked.

Blake looked down and I realized he might not want me to see where he lived before saying, "No, I like walking. Plus I don't live far." I wondered if he just didn't want me to see where he lived. I decided if that was the case, then I owed Blake whatever privacy he wanted.

I opened my car door, but didn't get in. "Well, this was the best date I've ever been on," I said truthfully.

Blake laughed. I figured he knew it was probably the only date I had ever been on. Instead of pointing that out he just leaned in and kissed me on the cheek before I knew what was happening. His lips were gentle and warm. I didn't move. I didn't speak. I seemed unable to do anything. Blake smiled and said, "I think it might be the best date I've ever been on too, Beth." With that he turned and left me standing by my car as he walked toward the edge of the parking lot, headed back toward the Quad.

After a minute that seemed like an hour, I came to my senses just enough to get in my car. I sat for a minute thinking. My whole world was so different from what it had been only a couple of weeks previously. My head swam in the clouds and I felt as if I was taking a calculus test on material I had never studied. I was used to knowing everything, even how I felt about everything. Now I was baffled and mixed up, but I felt like it was in a good way. How was this even possible? I drove home without thinking or even remembering driving. When I got home I could tell my mom was still up because the lights were on in the main room. I unlocked the door and went in to face the gauntlet.

My mom was sitting at the kitchen table, drinking out of a mug. She was pretending to read, but she wasn't fooling me. I could tell she had been waiting for me. I tried to slip by to walk up to my room, but she called out to me before I even reached the stairs. "Oh, you're home, Elizabeth. How was it?" she asked.

"Hi, mom. Sorry, I'm late," I apologized.

"You're not late," she responded. She looked at the clock on the wall above the table. It was shaped like the sun, and it showed that it was past 12:15. "You're right on time," she continued. "Do you want some hot chocolate?" she asked.

"On time for what? And no thanks," I replied.

"Oh, nothing," she said as if that was an answer. A slight grin crept up the corners of her lips. "Everything go okay?" she asked again.

"It was fine," I replied, not wanting to give up too much information. Usually, my mom and I talked about everything, but I wanted to keep my feelings and everything about Blake to myself. It was like he had trusted me and telling anything at all to someone else would be betraying that trust. "I'm going to go to bed," I said.

"Okay, sweetheart. See you in the morning," she replied.

After I got ready for bed and slid beneath the cool sheets, my mind replayed the events over and over. I could still feel the spot on my cheek where Blake had kissed me. This time, I could smell his clean soap smell--mixed with a kind of leather and cedar wood smell. As I drifted off to sleep, I wondered if I was remembering it or imagining it from a previous time. I decided I didn't care.

Chapter 3
Chocolate Milk Goes With Everything

The next morning was Saturday, of course. Although I was usually up by 5, I slept in until 7. I lay in bed after waking up and kept replaying everything through my mind. I checked my phone for a message just in case Blake had called or texted, but I didn't see anything except a text from Rebecca asking me to call her ASAP. I panicked for a minute when I realized I hadn't given Blake my number, but then I calmed down when I figured out there was nothing I could do about it and that I would probably see him on Monday to give him back his jacket.

I got up, still in my pajamas, and went downstairs. My mom and dad were sitting at the table. My Dad had a mug of coffee in front of him and was eating Raisin Bran out of a plastic bowl. He was still in his pajamas--a T-shirt, shorts, and bathrobe--and was looking at his laptop between bites. My mom had a tall glass of orange juice and had either already eaten or was skipping breakfast, which she often did. She was already dressed in black pants, red pumps, and a red blouse. She looked like she had been up for hours and was ready to head into the office where she used to work.

My mom reached over and took my dad's hand. He looked up as if he had been surprised before looking at her looking at him. He cleared his throat and said, "So, Elizabeth, how was the game?" So that was it, I thought to myself. She had failed to gain any information last night so she was trying again through my dad.

"It was fine," I replied. "We won 49 to 13." There was silence for a minute and my dad took another bite and returned his attention to his laptop until I noticed Mom squeezing his hand.

He looked up again and said, "49-13, huh? That quarterback, what's his name, must be pretty good." I had no idea how my mom and dad had figured out that I had gone out with Blake, but somehow they knew. My mom had always had some secret way of knowing everything. It was like she had a superpower or spies at school or something.

"His name is Blake," I offered, "and I guess he's pretty good. We haven't lost a game yet this year," I said.

He looked at me and then at my mom, not knowing what else to say. Finally, she let go of his hand and looked at me. "So what did you do after the game?" she asked.

"Just walked around with friends and stuff," I replied. It was kind of true, I told myself. "Nothing really."

"Nothing, really? Just walked around?" she asked as if implying she knew more.

I didn't fall for it. I knew some of her tricks at least. "Yeah, nothing too exciting. Just talked about the game and stuff," I lied. "Don't worry," I quickly added, "I didn't go to a party, and I didn't drink or anything."

My mom just looked at me like she thought her stare would break me. My dad was typing something on his laptop, probably revising some legal brief he needed to file. After a few minutes, my mom gave up and asked, "What are your plans today?"

"I need to call Rebecca and probably go over there to pick up something I left with her, and we'll probably study and read the chapters for science and calculus that will be covered this week," I replied.

"So, do you think you will go to any more games or walk around and talk about the game again anytime soon?" she asked.

I had thought I had thrown her off the scent, but it was clear she somehow knew exactly what was going on. I decided to play dumb. "Well, it was really fun going to the game and hanging out with Rebecca, so I'll probably go again sometime."

"Well, I'm glad you had a lot of fun hanging out with Rebecca," she said, slightly emphasizing the name Rebecca just to let me know I wasn't fooling her. How did she know? I wondered.

The rest of the morning was pretty quiet. I ate a bowl of half Frosted Flakes half Raisin Bran. My mom had gone shopping and I could have had my regular breakfast of Cheerios, but I liked the sugar of the Frosted Flakes mixed with the texture of the raisins. I could probably just add raisins to my Frosted Flakes, but somehow, I didn't think that would be the same. I went upstairs, showered and dressed, and got ready to go to Rebecca's. I quickly texted her, "Headed to your place soon. See you in a bit," and headed out the door after saying a quick goodbye to my mom and dad.

Rebecca only lives 15 minutes from me, but she lives in a gated community, so I had to go through a security gate, wait for them to check a list, and buzz me in through the gate. When I reached her house, I drove up the ridiculously long driveway to park next to her house since cars weren't permitted to park on the street in front of houses. Every time I came over, I thought about how glad I was that I didn't live here. Her house was very nice, but her neighborhood was haughty and condescending. Whenever someone looked at me in my blue Honda, a disdainful look followed me until I was out of sight.

Rebecca's house was a sprawling white stucco house with columns in front of the double red doors in front and a slate gray tiled roof. It had a 6-car garage on the left, where the driveway ended in a turnaround. Our house could easily fit inside half of her house, even without the garage. I parked at the turnaround so I wouldn't block any of the garage doors. The garage doors were fake polished wood that looked like they came off the dashboard of a Lexus. I walked around the brick sidewalk to the front doors and rang the doorbell. One time I had just knocked and opened the door and gone right in since I knew Rebecca was expecting me, but everyone was so shocked that I hadn't repeated that incident since then. Now, I always rang the bell because there had been times in the past when I had waited outside for a long time because nobody had heard my knocking.

Rebecca opened the door with a big smile on her face. I was glad the experience of the night before didn't seem to have had any lasting, negative impact on her. Inwardly I thanked Blake again, thinking that he was mainly the reason she was in such a good mood this morning instead of still shaken up.

"So?" she asked immediately when I had barely stepped through the door.

"What?" I responded, trying not to smile. I knew what she wanted, and she knew that I knew, but this little game was more fun than just telling her outright.

"Come on," she pleaded. What happened after I left last night?"

"Oh, that," I said, and she let out an exasperated sigh. "We just talked for a little bit, and then I came home." I tried to keep my voice expressionless, hoping she wouldn't be able to tell I was holding back. I wasn't exactly sure why, but I wanted to keep the details of the previous night to myself. I could trust Rebecca with anything, so it wasn't that I didn't trust her. It was more that Blake and I had shared a very personal experience with details not meant for anyone else. Telling her would feel like a betrayal to Blake, even though he hadn't said to keep anything secret. Honestly, I doubt he would mind if I told Rebecca, but still, I wanted to keep the details private.

"That's it?" Rebecca asked, discontented.

"Pretty much," I lied.

"I'm sorry," Rebecca said in a deflated tone. "It was probably my fault because of what happened with those boys."

I was beginning to feel bad for not opening up to Rebecca, but I still didn't feel right telling her everything. "Don't be silly," I said. "Last night was fun. We saw a great game, and neither of us was turned into vampires by the undead."

Her expression changed immediately. "Do you think those boys might have been vampires?" she asked.

A lot of times, I can't tell if Rebecca is really serious or if she is just taking her joke too far to see how much I believe. This was one of those times because I was pretty sure she was teasing, but she said it so seriously, and I knew if I called her out on it, she would pretend to be offended and feign outrage, so I played along like I usually did. "You never know," I replied back just as seriously. So, do you want to start with science, calculus, or something else?" I asked, trying to keep the subject off of last night.

"Definitely not calculus," replied Rebecca. "I know we have to go through it, but let's put that off as long as possible."

"Let's start with science then," I offered. "Mrs. Hart will probably have an extra hard test this week to make up for there not being one last week."

We headed to Rebecca's study room to work. She had her own office/study room right next to her bedroom, so she didn't have to have a desk in her bedroom. We passed her bedroom, which was painted a pale pink and had a queen-size walnut bed with a lavender comforter. I often wondered if she got lost in the bed. Her study room had two desks side by side and a table with four chairs around it, even though Rebecca and I were the only ones who were ever in there.

We sat at the table and opened up the science book to chapter 23. Our AP science class was split into two sections. The first half of the year, we had been studying physics, which went along with what we were covering in calculus. It seemed pretty basic to me because as long as you had a handle on calculus, physics seemed easy. Rebecca even picked up the formulas pretty quickly and it wasn't long before we were wrapping up the chapter. We had a system where we read the material and randomly worked three problems per page unless we had a very long theorem to prove, in which case we would just do one.

"You know," said Rebecca in a voice that seemed too sweet and innocent, "at the end of the quarter, we'll switch emphasis from physics to biology."

I wasn't sure what she was getting at. "Yeah, so?" I asked.

"So…do you think maybe Blake can help you learn biology?" she finished in a shriek of laughter.

"You are so hilarious," I said, looking around for something to throw at her. The moment passed with neither of us thinking of anything else to say so we went back to studying.

At 11:30, Rebecca declared that we needed to break for lunch. We went into the kitchen, and she started getting leftovers out of the refrigerator. I knew where everything was, so I made myself a peanut butter and apricot/pineapple jam sandwich and grabbed a box of Cheez-Its that Rebecca probably had her parents buy just for me. Rebecca heated up leftover salmon and crab cakes that her parents had probably brought home the night before. I had milk with my sandwich and cringed a little when she poured herself a glass of chocolate milk to have with her lunch.

"How can you drink chocolate milk with salmon and crab cakes?" I asked.

"Chocolate milk goes with everything," she replied as if that settled it.

After lunch, she opened a Tupperware container that had four shortbread cookies wrapped in a napkin. "Where did you get those?" I demanded. I could tell they were from the school's student store.

"I started buying some after school on Fridays to last me through the weekend," she explained. "You can have one if you want?" she offered.

I almost took one, even though I don't really like shortbread cookies, just to see her expression when her supply dropped. But then I remembered how scared she looked last night and how different people cope in different ways. Eating a cookie was much better than bottling everything up inside the way Blake had said his mom had done. I decided to let it slide since she had pretty much dropped her demand for details last night.

We finished lunch and went back to her study room for a couple more hours, reading through history/government, English, and finally calculus. Rebecca and I had different electives, so I couldn't really help her with her computer designing class, and she couldn't help me with my creative writing class. She also had an extra class that I didn't have--PE. I had taken 3 years, which was all that was required, so I didn't have to take it my senior year. Most students took it the first three years of high school and didn't take it their senior year. It was all I could do to maintain an A in PE, and I was glad to give up the morning jogs that I had done the first three years of high school in order to run the mile in under 7 minutes and maintain an A. I did kind of miss running with my mom in the mornings--not the running, just the time with her. Now she ran after I went to school and I felt a little guilty that she had to run alone, but not guilty enough to start running with her again.

Rebecca had elected to skip PE her freshman year--a decision she was now regretting. It was the only class she had a C in. She did any extra credit she could, but she still was barely passing. I knew it was killing her to have a C, but she just didn't like exercise, and the C she did have was kind of a gift from the teachers for picking up equipment every day at the end of class. Plus, she had it first period, which was the worst for PE because most students were still half asleep.

As we wrapped things up, I wondered if Rebecca would try to drill me again for details about last night. Sure enough, as soon as I put my last book in my backpack, she said, "So, what did you guys talk about last night?"

"Well, we wondered if you were okay after you left," I said, telling myself that was pretty much the truth. We did hope she was okay. We just didn't talk about her. "And we talked about the game," I lied easily now.

"So Blake was worried about me?" she asked. She seemed to pick up a glow, and I wondered if that was how I had looked when I came home last night. Maybe that was how Mom knew something had happened.

"Yeah, we both were. That was pretty awful," I said. To forestall any other questions, I quickly added, "Oh, and I need his jacket back."

Rebecca looked a little crestfallen. "I thought I could just bring it to school on Monday and give it to you then," she said. "Unless you're going to see Blake before then, maybe tonight?" she asked. I could tell she was hopeful for more information, but this time, there really was not anything to give.

"No, I'll see him Monday, but just in case I see him before you…"

"Okay," she said glumly. "I'll go get it." She went through the adjoining room to her bedroom, and I saw her reach under her comforter and pull it out. She had slept with it, I thought. I decided it was better to ignore that and not even mention it. She came back through the door and held it out to me.

"You don't have to leave right away," she said. My mom doesn't get back from her Yoga class until two, and my dad usually doesn't finish his rounds at the hospital until almost dinnertime." Her dad was a cosmetic surgeon. I had met him only a few times even though Rebecca and I had known each other for years. He hated the term "plastic surgeon" even though he did do a lot of augmentation surgeries. One of the only times we had talked about it, he had said that while a lot of his practice was implants, lip injections, and the like, he did it so he could work with burn victims, which he did for free. He did a lot of skin grafts, and I knew he was supposedly one of the best around at treating burns. And he also fixed cleft palates in young babies.

Rebecca's mom always seemed to be at yoga class or spin class, so whenever I was over to study, we were often alone. Rebecca's mom definitely didn't mind the sweat and exercise that Rebecca detested so much, but I could tell that exercise alone wasn't what made her look like the Barbie doll she resembled. Unlike Rebecca's dark brown hair, she had blonde hair with dark roots. The few times that I had met Rebecca's mom, she had been polite but standoffish as if she allowed her daughter to be my friend as long as I realized it was a sacrifice on her part. Rebecca's dad wasn't like that at all. He was warm and friendly. The few times I had met him and asked how he was doing, he launched into an explanation of the surgeries he had done that day or discussed how a burn patient was progressing. Rebecca always seemed embarrassed by her parents and felt like she had to rescue me from the conversations, but I thought her dad was great.

I had almost decided to stay when Rebecca brought up Blake again. "So, when are you going to see Blake again?" It was an innocent enough question, but if I wanted questions about dating, I already had a mom.

"I don't know," I replied. "We didn't really set anything up. Anyway, I'll see you on Monday," I said and started walking toward the door.

Too late, Rebecca realized her mistake. "We don't have to talk about Blake. We can talk about homework and quizzes," she prompted. She definitely knew me too well. I ended up staying another half an hour before Rebecca started hinting that she might need someone to walk her to her car after next week's game if I knew any football players who would be willing to." She was trying to hold in giggles when she said it, and I took it in good fun but still said my goodbye and headed home.

The rest of the weekend was pretty uneventful. I mostly stayed in my room and read *Pride and Prejudice* again, and every time I came out, my mom seemed to be there *just in case I wanted to talk about anything.*

On Monday, I got up extra early and left the house before 6, figuring I would eat breakfast at school just to avoid more conversation attempts by my mom at breakfast. I pulled into the school parking lot and I was the first car there. I always liked it when I was the first one at school-- like it was a contest I had won even though nobody else knew they were playing. This early, I knew there would likely not be any teachers here yet, except for Ms. Hart, who somehow was always here before me no matter how early I came.

I knew Rebecca wouldn't be here until close to 7, so I had about 30 minutes to myself. I could sit outside the library and read like I unusually did when I got to school early, but instead, I decided to walk around the Quad. I got to the Quad, and the grass was pretty damp with dew. It was starting to yellow since it typically went dormant over the winter. I was wearing blue jeans and a button up long sleeved top, but I hadn't brought a sweater since it was still warm in the afternoons. I had forgotten that it was getting cold in the mornings, and I was at the point of shivering by the time I reached the bench planter where Blake and I had sat on Friday night. I didn't really make a conscious decision to walk there. It was as if my feet moved on their own, and poof, I was there. I set down my backpack and books and half draped Blake's letterman jacket over my lap to add just a little warmth. I wanted to put it on, but I wasn't sure if I should since I didn't know if that gesture held some special significance, and even though it was unlikely I would be seen, I didn't want to give anyone the wrong impression. Wearing a boy's letterman jacket could have some serious meaning that I was unaware of.

I was deep in thought when I felt a presence right next to me. I turned, and Blake was standing 2 feet away from me, smiling and looking down at me. I was too surprised to be startled and was more dumbfounded, so like a moron, I just sat there mute while he stared, smiling down at me. Finally, he broke the silence. "You're here earlier than usual. It's good to see you."

I felt warmth spread through me when he said that. I couldn't help but smile back at him as he sat down next to me. I could smell the clean soap smell mixed with leather and cedar wood that I'd come to associate with him. His hair was slightly damp again, as if he'd just showered. He was wearing his usual plain black T-shirt, faded jeans, and checkered Vans. His Vans were slightly damp as were my shoes from the wet grass. When he sat down he set his backpack on the inside of the planter behind us and set his football next to it.

"You're here pretty early, yourself," I said.

"I always get here early," he replied. "The coach gave me a key so I can use the weight room and shower before school. But don't tell anyone. I'm not supposed to have a key," he explained.

"So you come here every morning this early?" I asked, surprised.

"Most mornings. Like I said, I try to be out of the house before my dad wakes up. Usually, he wakes up pretty late, but a few times, he's surprised me. I try not to let that happen anymore if I can help it."

The silence between us seemed to stretch. We both smiled, enjoying the moment. There was no sound of traffic, no crowds cheering or yelling, no masses talking in the background. There was only peaceful silence. This was better than studying for calculus, I thought. I thought I could be content to sit there until the morning bell rang, and it was time to go to class. The only sounds were occasional calls back and forth from birds in the trees around us. Everything else made me feel like we were in our own little world.

After what seemed like an hour, I realized I had Blake's jacket on my lap, and he had goosebumps all over his arms. He must be very cold, I thought. His hair was still damp, and he only had a thin shirt on. I handed him the jacket and said, "Rebecca said thanks so much. She seems fully recovered, in large part thanks to you."

"Kenny and Joey are trouble," he said. Devon's not too bad, but he's a follower and will do whatever the other two are doing. Tell Becca to watch out for them." The muscles of his jaw flexed as he spoke as if he were gritting his teeth in anger. His fingers gripped his jacket, and his biceps bulged a bit, becoming more prominent under his thin black shirt. After a minute, he relaxed. He slid his arms into the jacket, and I watched as he buttoned it up.

We sat for a while longer until Blake grabbed his backpack and football and stood up. "It's about 7:15. The student store and library will open soon."

I looked at my phone. It was 7:15. "How do you do that?" I asked.

"I'll walk you to the student store, and then I guess I'll let you get ready for your classes. I wouldn't want you to slip and get an A- on a test," he joked.

We started walking to the student store. I suddenly had a thought. "How come we're both seniors, and I've never seen you in one of my classes before?" I asked.

"Beth, you're in all the smart classes. I'm in the dumb jock classes," he said.

"But you're smart too," I protested.

"Not like you," he replied. "I could probably take some of the higher classes you take, but then I'd have to give up all the extra time I practice for football. As much as I don't like that people only see me as a football player, I'm more afraid I wouldn't be anything without football."

"That's not true," I argued. "You're very special. Anyone who took the time to get to know you would see that."

He smiled, and his big, crooked smile seemed to spread across his whole face. "I like you, Beth. Nobody knows me like you do. Nobody accepts me for anything but football. Thanks," he said. "Anyway, I was in a class with you. I can't believe you don't remember."

I racked my brain thinking about all the classes I'd attended the last three-plus years at Ridgeview High School. After just a couple of minutes, I gave up. "I'm sure if we were in class together, I'd have remembered it," I replied.

"Think back to Mrs. Benson's class, third grade," he said.

Immediately, I remembered a shy boy who came just before Christmas into my third grade class. He had no friends, and I felt sorry for him so I sat by him at lunch and on the bus a couple of times. We didn't talk much because he was pretty shy and he was only been in the class for three weeks. He looked so different, small, thin, and with a cast on his arm. "I remember you now," I said. "I can't believe that was you. Wait, you were only there for three weeks. What happened?" I asked.

"We moved around a lot. Until I got to high school, we probably moved four to five times a year," he said. "My dad didn't like staying in one place for too long," He explained without really explaining. I had a lot of questions running through my mind, but decided if he wanted me to know more, he would tell me.

We reached the pavement, and I could see Rebecca already waiting at the student store. She had a book open, and I was willing to bet it was a book about vampires and not a textbook.

Blake grabbed my hand and gave it a squeeze. "I'll see you later, Beth," he said. He released my hand slowly. I stopped to watch him walk back across the Quad toward the stadium.

When I turned back around, Rebecca was still standing in line with her head down in her book, oblivious to everything. I walked up to her quietly, thinking I would give her a good scare as a joke, but when I got 10 feet away from her, she looked up and said, "Hey, Elizabeth." We chatted as we waited for the store to open. She only bought one cookie today, and I bought two strawberry Appleway bars since I hadn't eaten breakfast. We walked to the library, again read through what we would be covering this week, and then headed for our first classes.

The day dragged by slowly. I had no tests and everything the teachers talked about, I already knew. I let my mind wander a few times and I started thinking about Blake. What did he see in me? I wondered. Was his home life really as bad as it sounded? Did he like me because I listened to him, or was he truly interested in me? He had kissed me, but that was on the cheek. My mind was a jumble of thoughts and I was glad Ms. Hart didn't have a surprise test for us. I knew I was in trouble because I had always looked forward to tests, especially from Ms. Hart, but now I was worried about the one she would surely "surprise" us with tomorrow. I decided I would really focus and review everything after school and be ready.

After school, I headed for the library. I was almost to the marble steps when I got a text from Rebecca. "Come to the parking lot NOW!"

That sounded desperate, so I half-walked and half-ran as fast as I could go with my heavy backpack and books. Twice, I dropped my books and had to stop and pick them up. The second time, I almost just left them.

I stepped off the curb across from the student parking lot and knew right away that something was wrong. Even though it was well after school and nearly everyone should be gone, the parking lot was full of kids standing around. They seemed to be grouped together. My breath caught as I nearly panicked, thinking of all the things it could be. Could Rebecca have been hit by a car? Could Joey or Kenny MacGruber--the two boys who attacked Rebecca after the game have come back and attacked her? My mind raced with negative thoughts as I squeezed my way through students. At one point, I broke through and there was a gap surrounding Rebecca and her Audi TTS. There was glass on the asphalt around her car and I could see the driver and passenger windows were broken out. The words *Rich Bitch* were spray painted on the driver's door, and deep scratches were etched into the glossy black paint marring its mirror finish. I walked up to Rebecca, who was visibly shaking and crying. She momentarily jumped a little bit when I put my arm around her shoulders.

"Who would do this?" she asked, her voice breaking just above a whisper. "Why?"

I looked around. Some students stood astonished but clearly entertained by the scene, and others were talking, laughing, and pointing. Somehow, near the back of the crowd, I detected two taller boys. One was tall had a reddish goatee, and a long neck. The other one was heavy set and a little older, but the resemblance between them was clear. Kenny and Joey weren't laughing or even talking, but both wore smirks, and I knew instantly that they were the ones who had done this. Kenny took a drag of his cigarette and then said something to his brother, who then laughed. I turned my attention back to Rebecca. "Is your car drivable, or do you want to call someone or just take my car?" I asked.

"I don't think I can drive right now," she replied. "Plus, two of my tires are flat. I called my dad, and he said he'll have someone come and tow it to a repair shop. Can we just leave?" I looked at the tires. I had overlooked them before because I was focused on the glass, spray paint, and scratches, but it was clear the front two tires had been slashed. Anger threatened to bubble up inside me, but I pushed it down, determined to remain calm for Rebecca.

"Of course," I replied. We started walking away, and I glanced through the busted driver's window. The black leather upholstery was cut up as if someone had stabbed and sliced it with a knife. Bits of glass were on the dash and seats. I realized I had missed that all four tires were flat--probably cut with a knife. We got to the crowd, and they parted for us. When we got to the edge of the parking lot, I saw Blake stepping off the opposite curb headed for us. He had a furious look on his face that scared even me. He was walking across the street toward us, but his gaze was focused over our heads to our left, and I knew he had spotted Joey and Kenny MacGruber.

He got to the parking lot and we stopped walking as he approached us. "Beth, Becca...are you two alright?" he asked in an almost gravelly whisper. Before we could even answer, he took a step past us, and I grabbed his arm. His eyes were deadlocked on Kenny and Joey. The muscles in his jaw were flexing and tightening as if they were already prepared to fight.

"We're fine, but you can do more help by staying with us and walking me to my car than by going after anyone," I said. I wasn't afraid for him even though they probably still had the knives they had sliced the tires with, and there were two of them. I was more afraid of Rebecca's emotional state. She was still shaking and visibly afraid. The fierceness left Blake's eyes as he turned and looked at Rebecca.

"Is she okay? Did she get hurt?" he asked.

Rebecca seemed to regain a little of her composure. "I'll be okay," she replied. "It's just a car."

I could tell she was still shaken. I held her hand as we walked toward my car. Her hand felt cold and trembled slightly as we walked. The crowd parted as Blake led us toward my blue Honda Civic. When we got there I unlocked the doors and helped Rebecca into the passenger seat. Blake stood staring off into the distance. I looked off in the direction he was gazing and could tell he was staring at Joey and Kenny MacGruber. Blake's jaw muscles flexed and he was gritting his teeth, anger turning his neck red. I grabbed his hand and squeezed it to get his attention.

"Hey, thanks for walking us to my car. Don't do anything stupid. Okay?" I asked. Blake continued to stare, his gray-blue eyes locked onto their target. I raised my voice, "Blake? They aren't worth it. We'll get it sorted out later."

He blinked and seemed to come back to himself. He turned and looked down at me. "Yeah, I'm just glad you two are alright." He turned his attention back to us, grabbed my hand, and gave it a quick squeeze before letting go. "I'll see you on Friday, after the game again?" he asked.

"Sure. I'll wait for you in the bleachers again, " I replied.

I got in my Honda and started the car. As I drove off, I could see Blake in my rearview mirror, staring in the direction of Joey and Kenny. I decided I couldn't do anything about Blake and turned my attention to getting Rebecca home. I could tell she was shaking and more upset than she let on. I tried to talk to her as we drove, but she just sat in silence as if she was in a trance. When we got to her house, I walked her to the door and her mom met us at the door. Her mom explained that Rebecca's dad was at the hospital but would be home later. We said our goodbyes, and I drove home. The ride home seemed especially silent.

The next morning I was still thinking about what had happened while sitting on the steps waiting for the library to open.

I decided to forgo any math or science since I doubted I could concentrate much on either, so I headed up to the fiction section 823.7. I scanned the shelves and found the book I was looking for fairly quickly. I decided to check it out and read outside instead of sitting at one of the tables like I usually did. When I came back to the desk where Mrs. Young was still scanning books, she stopped and looked up as if surprised someone would interrupt her. Perhaps she had forgotten that I was there. I placed the book on the counter next to her desk and she slowly reached for the book. She kind of did everything slowly and I had wondered many times if she worked in the DMV before becoming a librarian.

"Pride and Prejudice by Jane Austin. Good choice," she rasped. I had never seen her smoke, but her voice definitely had the scratchy depths of a lifelong smoker. I grunted something that could have been an affirmation, and she scanned the book. "This says you were the last person to check this out," she stated in an almost accusatory tone. "In fact, it says you were the last three people to check it out. It says you checked it out twice this year and 3 times last year. If you aren't able to finish it in two weeks' time, I can always renew it. In fact, since you're probably the only one who checks this out, I can check it out for four weeks instead of two if you need me to. "Uh, no thanks.

Two weeks is fine…one week even," I replied. She looked at me doubtfully as she scanned and stamped the book. Her pale, grayish-toned skin looked a bit milky under the glow of the fluorescent lighting. I had been in here every single day since coming here, and many days, I was in here before school, during lunch, and after school. How could she think I needed more than two weeks to read a book that I had read many times before? I was a bit indignant at the thought, as if she were somehow questioning my intelligence or motivation. Brain power and dedication were about the only things I had going for me. Except now I had something else possibly. What exactly was it, I pondered.

I went over the events and conversation again in my head as I slowly descended the marble stairs. I often would replay events over and over in my head, trying to figure out if there was something I could have said or done differently. My dad says I'm like him because I overanalyze everything. After a test, I replay every answer, every sentence, every word over and over in my head, thinking about different ways I could have answered and wondering if I should have done anything differently. When I get back test results, it's not just another A for me; it's a validation of who I am and a confirmation that all the time I spent studying was the right decision. I usually agonize over everything until I find out how I did on a test, even though I always get an A.

Chapter 4
Shove It In Their Faces

The next day, Rebecca wasn't at school. I texted her to make sure she was alright, and she said she was just taking a personal day and that everything was okay. I made it to all my classes but didn't see Blake at all. My time in the library seemed especially lonely that afternoon, and I had a difficult time concentrating on my calculus notes from Mr. Jennings's class earlier in the day, even though I knew Rebecca would need my rewritten notes when she got back.

The next morning, I pulled into the parking lot early, determined to catch up on the studying I had slacked on the day before. There was only one other car in the parking lot, a car I had never seen before. I stared in disbelief at a black Hummer H3 convertible parked in the exact spot where Rebecca's car had been parked. There was still glass in the parking lot around it from Rebecca's Audi. Surely Rebecca wouldn't have gotten this monster of a car just to show off, I thought. Rebecca wasn't the type to show off. Her family had money, but she just drove what she drove because she liked what she liked. This was definitely a statement.

I walked to the student store and spotted Rebecca standing in line, as always, waiting for it to open. "Rebecca, tell me you didn't," I said.

"Hi, Elizabeth," she replied as if not hearing what I had said.

"Rebecca, you can't be serious. That car is just going to piss them off more and make an even bigger target," I said.

"Oh, you noticed my new car? It's just until the Audi is fixed. Daddy thought I should drive something safe, and it has a high safety rating."

"Seriously, you don't think it's dangerous? You don't think you're tempting fate?"

"People like that are going to be jealous no matter what I drive, so why not?" she replied.

I had to hand it to her. She got over her scare from two days before pretty quickly.

The student store opened and Rebecca stepped up as the window slid open. To my surprise, she ordered 3 Appleway bars and an orange juice, then handed one of the bars to me.

"No cookie today," I asked. "Are you feeling okay?"

"I'm great," she replied. I'm just not going to live in fear anymore. Anyway, you always eat these things, and you got Blake, so I thought I'd try one."

"I don't HAVE Blake," I countered. "We've just hung out a couple of times. Anyway, you know these have nothing to do with it."

"I know, but I thought I needed a change. I was stuck in the same routine, and I was reminded that sometimes a change is good."

I had to hand it to Rebecca. She was handling this much better than I thought possible. We ate our breakfast together and walked to the library. She told me about all the anti-theft and anti-vandalism features of her Hummer. It had theft notifications that would text Rebecca if anyone was messing with it and mini cameras built in that would record any vandalism attempts, and a voice that would warn anyone who got too close that they were being recorded. It certainly seemed like Rebecca's new confidence was well-founded. We went over the notes from the day she had missed and agreed to meet for lunch. The day flew by, and we were walking to the library during lunch when Blake popped up out of nowhere. He had the ability to always just be there. I never seemed to see him walking up to us; he was always just there one minute where he hadn't been before.

"Hey, Beth; hey, Becca. I love your new car, Becca," he said as he smiled. "That's really shoving it in their faces. Good for you!"

I wanted to argue with him and tell him I thought it was foolish, but after looking at his smile and the reaction his words had on Rebecca, I bit back my words. Rebecca beamed, but she said what I didn't. "You don't think it's too much? I don't want to draw too much attention," she said.

"No, really," he added. "Why should you live as a victim because some losers are jealous?"

This made Rebecca smile even bigger and so it made me feel better. We went to the library and sat at our usual table. Blake came with us but just sat and watched us go over notes from Mrs. Hart's science class. Mrs. Young, the librarian, pepped right up when she saw Blake, and she somehow remembered his name this time.

After lunch, Blake said he would meet Rebecca after school to walk her to her car before hurrying to practice, and then he would meet me at the library after football practice to walk me to my car. This continued the rest of the week until Friday, when Blake said he wouldn't be able to meet us because he had to get ready for the game after school.

By Friday, Rebecca was back to eating a cookie from the student store each morning, but to her credit she was only eating one a day as far as I could tell. Since I knew this was her coping mechanism, I figured she was doing pretty well. We agreed to meet at the stadium so I went home right after school, skipping the library for the afternoon.

I had been spending time every day with Blake, so even though this was technically our second date, it didn't feel like it. I laid out a lacy blue cotton blouse with sleeves that went just past my elbows and oval cutouts at the shoulders. It was warm enough for outside if we went to the Quad to talk, but cool enough so I wouldn't be sweltering if we went to a dance or party. All I had left to do was change, but by the time I had changed, I noticed an hour had passed. I had no idea where the time had gone, but I had told Rebecca I would meet her at 5:30, so I hurried downstairs to go.

Before I could leave, my mom reminded me to call her if I needed a ride and not to drive if I had been drinking. I laughed when she said this because I never drank. She seemed to think that I needed to lighten up and spend my high school years having more fun like she did when she was in high school. I never understood why she didn't go to college, but I think it had to do with getting pregnant pretty much right out of high school and getting married right away. She said she had no regrets and that she just wanted to make sure I didn't have any, but I often wondered if there was more to it than that.

I got to the game and saw Rebecca's Hummer H3 was already in the parking lot. I made my way through the tunnel to the concrete stadium and over to the right, where Rebecca was already waiting. We talked and ate as we waited for the game to start, and just like the time before, my mind kept wandering to speculation and daydreams of what would happen after the game.

Blake had said we could go get a burger at Getaburger, we could go to a party he knew about, or we could just hang out and talk like last time. If possible, I was even more nervous than the last time. If we went to a party, we would see all of Blake's friends, including cheerleaders. *How could I compete with them?* I wondered. On the other hand, if we just sat and talked again, would Blake get bored with me or expect more? This was only our second date and even though we had been spending more time together during the week, we still barely knew each other. Blake didn't seem like the pushy type, but I also knew that all of this was uncharted territory for me. It wasn't like I had any experience with past boyfriends to compare to. Blake was the first boy I had ever dated. I trusted Blake, but I wasn't sure I completely trusted myself. Going out for burgers after the game seemed the safest venture.

The game flew by, with Blake throwing three touchdown passes and running in for two more. The audience cheered louder with each one, and I was caught up in the sense of school pride everyone--especially Rebecca--shared collectively. Rebecca had on her school T-shirt with the Ridgeview Wildcats logo on it. She also had her foam Wildcats seat to sit on, but most of the time, she was standing and cheering with the crowd. I saw a few others around us with foam seats but no students. Mostly, older people seemed to be the ones with the seat cushions.

By the end of the game, we had eaten the Nachos and soft pretzels Rebecca had bought, along with a couple of cokes and hot dogs. So much for going out for burgers afterward.

The game ended, and people started filing out of the stadium. Rebecca waited since Blake had said we should both wait for him so he could walk her to her car. The stadium was nearly empty, and I looked around at the few people milling around while we waited for Blake to come out. My eyes caught on two dark figures standing at the base of the visitor's metal bleachers. I couldn't tell who they were, but the heavier set of the two was smoking. I could just make out enough of them in the shadows to see that they looked like they were staring at us. The larger one--presumably Joey--would take a drag of his cigarette while staring in our direction while the other one would look around nervously as if on the lookout for someone.

I jumped just a little a second later when Blake touched my arm in greeting. He had just appeared like he always seemed to do. One minute he wasn't there, and the next he was.

"Hey, Beth. Hey, Becca. Everything okay?" he asked.

"Everything is great," replied Rebecca. "Great game."

"Thanks," Blake replied.

I looked back over at where Joey and Kenny MacGruber had been but couldn't see them anymore. They must have moved off, but I was sure it had been them.

As Blake walked Rebecca to her car, I kept looking around, expecting to see them. We got to Rebecca's H3, said our goodbyes to Rebecca, and watched her drive off. I turned and looked at Blake expectantly, wondering what we would do next.

"So there's a party at Rory's house but it's too early to go still. That means we can hang out here or go get a bite to eat," he said.

"I don't mind going out, but I'm not hungry. Sorry, but we ate during the game."

"That's okay," he replied. "I can't really eat after a game anyway. Too much adrenaline still going on. It takes about an hour to wind down."

"We can just hang out in the Quad and go to the party later," I suggested. "Will a lot of your friends be there?"

"Yeah, I'm not really into parties, but I have to put in an appearance. It's dumb, but people expect to see me there. For some reason, if I don't show up at someone's house, someone will think I'm mad at them or jump to some other ridiculous conclusion. It's no big deal. There's loud music and drinking and some people might be smoking, but nobody is pushy. I'm not really into the drinking and partying that a lot of them are into. Maybe because I see where it leads…with my dad, I mean."

We continued talking as we made our way to the same little planter bench where we had sat before. I admired how Blake seemed to be able to open up and talk about anything. He seemed so comfortable while I was always running everything I said through a dozen filters first to make sure it was worded just right. Blake made me forget my caution and want to open up. I felt like I could be myself around him without worrying about how it would come across or who I might offend if I didn't word it precisely right.

"Your dad drinks a lot?" I asked before I knew what I was saying.

A dark and serious expression came over Blake as his brow drew down. "Yeah. He drinks a lot. Every day, he drinks a lot. He says he drinks because of my mom leaving us, but he drank a lot even before that. I don't ever remember a time when he wasn't drunk or on his way."

"I'm sorry," I said. "I shouldn't have even brought it up. It's none of my business."

I tried to think of something to add, but before I could think of something else to say, Blake answered. "It's okay. It feels good to talk to someone about it. For some reason, I feel like I can just open up to you. The people at school they don't seem to care about anyone or anything but themselves. They're all caught up in what they will be doing the next weekend after the game, but they don't ever think about anything else," he finished.

I thought back to the little boy I had first seen in third grade. I had only known him for less than three weeks. Since Blake had reminded me of our first encounter, I had remembered vividly how shy and scared he had been, but I also remembered his smile when I sat by him at lunch or on the bus. It didn't seem like he had changed all that much. He was very popular now but still shy and closed off.

Except he had opened up to me. He had trusted me. I didn't know what to do, so I reached out and grabbed his hand. His large hand was warm in mine and I could not even wrap my fingers all the way around his. He smiled at me, and we just sat there. Neither of us felt like we had to say anything. We were just comfortable sitting there holding hands.

After a while he began to tell me about some of the places he had moved. It was strange listening to someone talk about moving every 3-4 months--sometimes only staying at a place for a few weeks. While listening to Blake talk about his dad changing jobs and them moving half a dozen times a year, I felt a little guilty, having lived in the same house for my entire life. Blake's dad did odd jobs and jumped from job to job often. He was a night watchman at a mall for a few months at one place, a nighttime custodian at a hospital for a few weeks, a mechanic who fixed flat tires and mufflers…There were so many jobs, more often at night and alone, and I wondered how Blake had adjusted so well in such an unstable environment. Since Blake had entered high school, his dad had managed to keep the same job for four years--a handyman for an apartment complex. This allowed Blake to stay at the same high school and join the football team. He made varsity his freshman year, which at first ruffled a lot of feathers since he was competing with other kids who had played club football for private clubs for years, and Blake had just picked it up. He was a natural athlete who was able to focus and put everything into the moment. He said he had learned to appreciate each moment and put everything into whatever he was working on at the time because most things in his life were temporary and short-term. He loved football but didn't like that everyone started thinking of him as just a dumb jock who was only good at throwing a football.

Blake also liked art history and even liked writing. He was obviously smart, and the fact that he was able to maintain good grades--while not in the top AP classes--

after such a disruptive and inconsistent school experience when younger showed just how quick-witted he was. He was able to read the field and change a play the instant something went wrong or wasn't working. He was also able to read a chapter in his history book, remember everything he read, and ace a test without studying. As sharp as he clearly was, he was surprisingly modest and humble.

I glanced at my watch, and Blake said, "It's just past 10:30." My watch read 10:33.

"How do you do that?" I asked.

"I don't know. It's just a trick," he said. Like everything else, he seemed to not take credit for something he could do that others couldn't. He just seemed to take it for granted. "Did you want to head over to the party? It's at Rory's house. His parents are out of town."

"Sure," I said. "Whatever you want to do."

He asked if I minded driving because he had to share his dad's truck and didn't have it that night. We made our way to the parking lot. My blue Honda Civic was the only car left in the parking lot, and we continued talking as we made our way to it and then to Rory's house which Blake had to give me directions to as I drove.

We parked down the street because the street was full of parked cars. We could hear music pounding as we walked to the house, but not blaring loud. Blake explained that he usually didn't stay past 11:30, and if the music was too loud, he left early because there had been times when the cops had busted up parties.

The door was open, and people were spilling out onto the steps and lawn. I could smell beer and cigarette smoke as we walked up the driveway. When we got to the doorway, we had to step over a boy who was sitting down with his legs stretched out in front of him, beer in hand. As soon as we entered, people started calling out Blake's name. He would nod to them or shout out their name above the roaring music that was blaring from somewhere. The music had been only loud outside, but inside, it was blasting, and I could feel my teeth rattling slightly.

We made our way to the living room, which was packed with so many people that I couldn't even tell what color the carpet was. The smells of beer, sweat, cigarette smoke, and what must have been pot were so strong it burned my nose if I breathed in too deeply, so I tried to keep my breathing slow and shallow. Blake leaned in and said something in my ear, but I couldn't hear what he said so he leaned in and shouted right in my ear, "You doing okay?"

I looked up at him and shouted, "Yes!" while nodding in case he couldn't hear me. He grabbed my hand and pulled me through the crowd. As we wove through the crowd, people kept slapping Blake on the back and calling out to him. He would nod back or give fist bumps. We got to the kitchen, where the crowd was moving in and out toward a counter that held a keg. Blake grabbed two red solo cups and filled each one halfway up with beer from the keg.

"You don't have to drink this," he said. "Just hold it, or people will keep trying to give you more." The music was still loud in the kitchen, but I could hear Blake, who only had to talk slightly louder than normal in order to be heard.

A tall, thin blond kid stepped up and clapped Blake on the shoulder before fist-bumping him. "Blake, glad you made it."

"Wouldn't miss it, Rory," Blake replied.

Rory had freckles on his face, neck, and hands. His eyelashes matched his blond hair. He was as tall as Blake, but his shoulders were about half as wide as Blake's. He was thin enough that I could tell just from looking at him that he wasn't on the football team.

A short, curvy girl came up behind Rory as we stood there and wrapped her arms around his waist. He turned half around and put his arm around her shoulders. She was thin and pretty in a cheerleader sort of way, but she definitely was not a cheerleader. Her hair was jet black, as dark as Rory's hair was light, but had a streak of dark blue running through it. She was wearing blue jean shorts even though it was a chilly night outside. Her red sweater showed an ample amount of cleavage, and she had a big, friendly smile on her face.

"Rory, this is Beth," Blake said, nodding his head in my direction. Rory nodded in my direction and pulled the girl around next to him.

"Perla, say hi to Beth," Rory said. The girl looked over at me and smiled even bigger.

"Hi, Beth," Perla replied. Her voice was low and gravelly. It sounded scratchy, as if she had been yelling a lot and was on the verge of losing her voice. She grabbed my hand away from Blake's and squeezed it.

I squeezed it back and smiled in return.

Blake leaned down and said, "I gotta talk to Rory for a minute. Will you be alright here for a minute?"

I nodded, and he grabbed Rory by the elbow and nodded to his right. The two walked off a little ways but were still in the room. I could see them talking but couldn't hear anything they were saying. Every few seconds, Rory would look over at me and nod. I couldn't tell what they were talking about, but it sure felt like I was involved in their conversation. I took a sip of the beer. It was warm and didn't taste good at all to me, so I set it on the counter.

Perla leaned in, and my attention shifted back to her. I could tell she was about to say something. "So how do you know Blake?" she asked.

"We, umm, just started talking and hanging out one day," I replied.

"Well, I'm impressed," Perla remarked. "In the three years I've known him, lots of girls have tried to get with him--including most of the cheerleaders--but I've never seen any of them have any success. To be honest, I was beginning to think he might be gay. No judgments, you understand, but a guy that good-looking, not hooking up with any of the tons of girls who throw themselves at him…Do you know what I mean?" her voice trailed off.

I felt my cheeks grow hot with embarrassment, but I also felt a little pride creeping in. "I don't know," I answered. "I guess we just understand each other." As I said this, I realized this was true but that it took me saying it out loud to even realize it. It was like I must have understood it in my heart, but my mind hadn't yet caught on. Blake and I hadn't known each other for very long, but we understood each other. We trusted each other. We fit. That's all there was to it. We fit.

I looked up, and Perla was looking at me through long black lashes, the kind that are a pain to glue on but look fabulous once you do. She had an expression that showed comprehension and awareness, as if she knew exactly what I meant.

"That's exactly what I feel with Rory," she explained. "I mean, we both have been with lots of other people, and we are totally different from each other, but somehow, when we met, we just knew. There was a kind of connection. We didn't have to try to pretend to be somebody else. We could just relax and be ourselves, which is rare because, just between you and me, most of these people are so fake."

With that statement, I could tell why Blake liked Rory and Perla. They were genuine people. Blake was great at reading people. He could probably instantly tell who was fake and who was real, and Perla just said most of the people here were fake. They were pretending to be what they thought would make them popular. I was starting to see why Blake had seemed so lonely. I at least had Rebecca. She went to games and wore shirts to try to fit in, but mostly, she was real. For the most part, she didn't fit in and she was okay with that. She didn't hide who she really was. She wasn't afraid to talk about her obsession with vampires. She didn't care that she was a smart nerd who got almost all A's. I didn't hang out with a lot of other people so I just thought everyone was like Rebecca and me, and Blake. I didn't know that so many people were putting on a masquerade. Many people at school wore a costume of who they wanted people to see and never let anyone see the real person they were. Maybe they had worn the mask and pretended for so long that they didn't even know who they really were anymore.

As I was thinking about this, Blake and Rory came back over. Perla put her arms around Rory's midsection and clung to him as if he had been gone for weeks. Blake leaned down and asked if I was ready to go.

"Already?" I asked. "We just got here."

"We can stay if you want," he stated.

"No, I'm ready. I just thought you would want to stay and hang out with your friends," I responded.

"I don't really like to hang out where people are drinking. Most of these people are just going to get bombed until they puke. That's not really my thing, as you know. I mostly come so people don't get mad at me and think I slighted them. If that happens, then drama starts happening, and the next thing you know, they aren't blocking like they should be, and I get tackled during the next game. It's dumb, but I've learned to just go with it and placate people. Anyway, don't you have to be home by midnight?"

When he said this, I checked my watch. It was 11:25. How did he do that? I wondered. "I don't HAVE to be home by then, but my parents probably wouldn't be happy if I came home super late," I said. Perla and Rory were looking at me oddly and I realized they probably weren't used to being around someone who cared about getting in trouble or who worried about what parents thought.

I was slightly self-conscious and uncomfortable under their stares until Blake fist-bumped Rory and said, "Later." Perla grabbed my hand and squeezed it as she smiled. I smiled back and felt at ease again. Blake grabbed my hand, and we started making our way toward the front of the house. Once we were in the main room, the music grew louder again, and we began squeezing our way through the mass of people. Just before we reached the front door, a very drunk, red-headed boy turned and bumped hard into me, the beer in his red solo cup splashing all down the front of my shirt and partially down onto my pants. Blake stepped forward and gave him a shove.

"Watch it, Danny," he semi-shouted so he could be heard above the music. The boy staggered back a couple of steps. He was a couple of inches shorter than Blake, but he was much heavier.

He took a step toward Blake, swaying back and forth slightly. "Why don't you watch it?" he replied in a slurry voice. He looked at Blake, and I thought there would be a big problem, but then he seemed to recognize Blake and apologized, "Sorry, man. My fault," he hiccupped as he spoke.

Blake pulled me toward the door, and soon, we were stepping over the person who was still sprawled across the doorway. Once we were outside, we started walking across the grass to my car. The music was still poundingly loud, but outside, it was slightly muffled. We could hear each other but still had to raise our voices to a near yell.

"Are you okay?" Blake bellowed.

"Yeah, I'm fine," I hollered back. "Just a little damp." The warm beer that had spilled down my blue cotton blouse had soaked down to my skin and had begun to turn cold with the outside air. My pants were also damp but not as saturated as my top. The smell of beer permeated me, and as we got into my Honda, I hoped the dampness from my pants wouldn't soak into the fabric of the seats and make the car smell like beer. The moisture created a clamminess that made my blouse cling to my skin. Most of the wetness was on my top and the front of my jeans and I decided it didn't matter if some soaked into the upholstery. There was nothing I could do about it. I would just have to deal with that later.

"Sorry about that," Blake apologized once we were in the car and driving away. "Normally, it doesn't get that bad until later. That's why I usually don't hang around long."

"It's okay," I replied. "It'll dry. Where should I take you?"

Blake was quiet for a minute before saying, "Just take me back to school, and I'll walk home from there."

"Don't be silly. I'll drive you to your house. Front door service," I joked. I could tell Blake was uncomfortable. He probably didn't want me to see his house. "Don't worry. I don't care where you live," I said.

"It isn't that," he started. "Well, that's part of it, but I don't want you to be at my place in case my dad is home. He's usually passed out by now, but sometimes he's still up, and he's a pretty mean drunk. How about you just drop me off in front of the apartment complex?" I could tell Blake was embarrassed having to say this and that there was more, but he didn't want to have to say it.

"That sounds like a plan," I replied. Blake gave me directions, and we drove to an older apartment complex a few miles east of the school.

When we got to the apartments, Blake hesitated and didn't get out right away. He looked down at his hands, which were in his lap, and the moment seemed to drag on. Neither of us wanted the night to end. It wasn't a perfect night by any stretch of the imagination, but I had begun to value every minute we spent together. Finally, he leaned over and kissed me right on the lips. It was a soft and tender kiss at first. It seemed to stretch on but was way too brief. When he pulled back, he seemed almost as surprised as I was. Maybe what Perla had said was true, and Blake hadn't had a string of girls. She had said many had tried but that he had avoided them. I had thought that maybe she just said that because he hadn't hooked up with her, but maybe he hadn't connected with any of the girls at school. He had said once that all the popular girls at school were empty shells with nothing to offer. He had called them shallow and had said that he couldn't talk to any of them. I didn't know what to think at the time, and honestly, I still didn't completely understand.

"Thanks for tonight. For listening earlier, and I'm sorry about the beer. Next time, we'll go somewhere nice and quiet."

I was still too flustered from the kiss to say much, so I just mumbled, "That would be nice."

"I'm afraid you won't make it home until after midnight. It's ten til now," he said.

"That's okay," I replied. "My mom has always been real understanding. She actually tells me to go out more and have fun."

"Must be nice. Anyway, see you Monday," he said and got out. After he shut the door, he lingered, so I rolled down the window, not knowing what to expect. He didn't have any of the usual confidence and seemed to hesitate before leaning down to look through the window.

"I don't want to scare you," he started, "but I think I'm falling for you." With that, he stood up and I watched as he walked away. I couldn't have been more overwhelmed and stunned by what he had said. I realized at that moment that I was also falling for him if I hadn't already.

I watched him go as long as I could and couldn't help but notice the difference in our living conditions. The sidewalk was cracked and tree roots had pushed it up in places. There was tagging on the dirty yellow stucco of the apartment building and what little grass remained was littered with broken pieces of various plastic toys, a bent-up rim of a bicycle wheel, and a rusted-out barbeque sat on a slab of concrete partially blocking someone's door. I felt a little guilty as I drove away, but at the same time, I felt warm and more content than I think I ever had.

Chapter 5
Mom, It's The Truth!

It was 20 minutes before I pulled into my driveway. I had rolled down the windows and let the air wash over me as I drove to try to dry my blouse. My clothes were somewhat dry as I walked through my front door, still thinking about the warm pressure of his lips on mine. My mom was sitting at the kitchen table reading a book and looked up as I came in.

"Hey, hon. How was your date?" she said.

I started to answer, but she abruptly cut me off. "Elizabeth, is that beer I smell?"

I answered before I even thought about it, "Yes, but it's not mine." Somehow, I thought that would explain everything, but I could tell by the expression on her face, the redness creeping up her neck, that it had only made things worse.

"So you and Blake were, what, drinking and partying after the game, and then you drove home after drinking?" by the time she finished the sentence, she was talking as loudly as if she had been in the house with us and the blaring, pounding music. I tried to get ahead of this and calm her down.

"Mom, it's not what you think. We weren't drinking," I began before she cut me off again.

"So you smell like a brewery because you weren't drinking?"

"No, yeah," I began. "Others were drinking, and someone spilled their beer on me. I got all wet--drenched, actually."

"And then you drove home after drinking? Why didn't you call us for a ride?" she continued as if I hadn't said anything. "You know we always tell you to call us if you need a ride home. And now, you're lying to me on top of it?"

"Mom, it's the truth. We weren't drinking. We stopped by a house where people were drinking, but we didn't drink at all," I tried to explain.

"So you're saying you didn't drink at all?" she asked disbelievingly. "You say you were drenched, but you look pretty dry to me. Let me smell your breath," she demanded.

I stepped forward, eager to prove my innocence, but instantly remembered that I did have a sip when I was talking to Perla. *Would one small drink be enough to smell on my breath?* I wondered. I decided to be completely honest before my mom became even angrier. She had always been very reasonable and supportive in the past. At least, I thought so.

"Okay, I had a sip of beer, but not enough to matter," I started.

"So you just lied again," she exclaimed brusquely. "First, you say you didn't drink at all, but now you say you did drink, but that you can handle drinking and then driving home." I could tell her temper was rising with each passing second. Her face was flush with irritation. I wanted to explain more, but I was afraid anything I said would just provoke her even more. She had always been so rational and sensible in the past. Hadn't she been the one to say I needed to go out more and enjoy my youth while I was still young?

I decided to take a different approach. I knew there was probably no way I would be able to explain away her temper and that if I tried, it would likely just rub her the wrong way and inflame her temper even more.

"Mom, I'm sorry. We really weren't drinking much, and anyway, it won't happen again. I promise."

"You're right. It won't happen again. You're grounded. Next week, you are to come straight home after school. You will not be going to the game next weekend or anywhere else. You are not to see or talk to Blake while you are grounded. That may become permanent. I am going to talk to your dad about this," she threatened. "This quarterback, Blake, seems like a bad influence on you."

Indignation began to rankle me. I knew I should have kept calm, but I couldn't help myself. "We didn't do anything wrong!" I yelled. I could now feel my cheeks heating with anger.

"Let's make it two weeks," she replied.

Now, she was quiet and calm, icy. She was back in control of herself, but I could still tell by her eyes that she was extremely ticked off. We had never fought like this before, but somehow, I knew that nothing I said would change her mind. I looked at her and it was as if I was looking at a stranger. She had always been the one who supported me, defended me even. Now, I felt as if she had cut my legs out from under me. How dare she blame me for something that was out of my control? I had done nothing wrong, nor had Blake, for that matter. I felt defensive and was so angry at her blaming Blake that the corners of my vision started to dim as I started getting tunnel vision. All I could see was my mom judging Blake and me. It felt so unfair, so unjust. I could feel tears start to well up, and my eyes stung as I blinked them away.

Without another word, I stomped up the stairs to my room. I buried my head in my pillow. I was exhausted but too angry to sleep, so I just lay on my bed in my dirty clothes until sometime in the night, I drifted off, and a restless sleep overtook me.

Chapter 6
So Unfair!

When I woke up the next morning, I was bad-tempered and still fatigued. I should have been dreaming of kissing Blake all night and woke up feeling his hand holding mine, his lips pressing on mine. Instead, I had dreams of my mom's irritated, pinched face as she grounded me over and over. In my dreams, she kept saying what a bad influence Blake was and how I needed to stop seeing him and find a respectable boy with a decent background.

I had slept in my clothes, and the first thing I noticed was that I still smelled really bad. I could smell both beer and the odor of pot on my clothing. I knew they had been smoking pot at the party last night, but I didn't realize its odor had permeated my clothing to such an extent. No wonder my mom was so angry. I decided I would shower, dress, and then go downstairs to apologize and plead my case.

I threw my clothes in the washing machine so my mom wouldn't smell them and be affronted again by the smell. I had to start thinking of a way to mellow my mom's mood so that I could get her to see reason and lift my punishment. Unfortunately, it was too late to get up early and make her breakfast. As I thought about it, that would have been the way to go, but I had slept in, so my mind raced to try to come up with a plan B. I couldn't go a week, maybe two, without seeing Blake or going to the library. I was sure I could convince her to relent if I just could come up with the right words to persuade her that I really hadn't done anything wrong. In fact, I was kind of following her advice to loosen up and enjoy my senior year. Hadn't she said again and again that there was more to life than books?

I was determined to plead my case as I walked downstairs and entered the kitchen. At the bottom of the stairs, I could hear my mom and dad talking in soft tones before I came around the corner into the kitchen. The conversation stopped as they both looked at me, and I paused before coming the rest of the way into the kitchen. Although it was Saturday, my dad was dressed in a white dress shirt with a red striped tie and black slacks. He was obviously heading back to work like he often did on Saturdays. He always said it was just a couple of hours to catch up on something, but he would usually spend half the day there. The fact that he hadn't left yet told me they considered what had happened to be serious. Mom had a stern expression as she peered at me over her cup of orange blossom tea. She drank coffee and usually only had tea on Sundays, but I could see the bag draped over the edge of the cup. I didn't know what it meant--that she had broken her routine--but figured it couldn't be good for me.

"Good morning, Mom, Dad," I started as I edged my way the rest of the way into the kitchen.

Dad looked up from his paper and grunted something that sounded kind of like, "G'mornin." My mom just glowered without saying a word. Soon, the silence seemed to stretch to infinity. It was clear if the ice was to be broken, it would have to be by me.

"So, uh, I was hoping we could talk," I began.

Silence. More staring.

"About last night," I continued. "I think there was a misunderstanding."

That was as far as I got.

My dad broke in, "Misunderstanding? So you weren't drinking, and you didn't drive home afterward?" he said in a low undertone. When my mom was angry, she raised her voice and even yelled sometimes, though, before last night, it had been a rare occasion when she had done so. My dad, on the other hand, lowered his voice to a murmuring sough. Throughout my seventeen years, I had very rarely even seen him upset, but the few times I had told me that this time topped them all.

"Not really," I started. "If I could just explain."

"Not really?" my mom broke in. "Elizabeth, don't start with that double speak that you tried to pull last night. You lied last night, and you were caught. Don't compound the trouble you're in by lying again."

I could tell this was not going as I had hoped. Maybe it was even going worse than last night, if that was possible.

"And what about the pot?" my dad came back. "Your mom said she could smell it on you, that you reeked of it last night. Are you going to try to sell us on you drank but you didn't drink? You smoked pot, but you didn't smoke pot? You drove home high and drunk, but it was okay because you said...what was it...that you could handle it?" His nostrils flared as he talked, and his eyebrows lowered together, making creases that formed a V just between his eyes.

I could tell he was furious--possibly more angry than I had ever seen him before. I began to feel bile rising in my throat as anger and indignation rose up in me. This was completely unfair, I thought. I hadn't done anything wrong. Not really. Why were they jumping to conclusions without even hearing my side of things? I took a slow, deep breath to calm myself and tried again.

"Okay, you have the wrong idea about what happened," I said, keeping my voice calm and even. "Blake and I went to a party, but we didn't smoke or drink or anything. We only stayed a little while." I was trying to talk in soothing tones, but I realized it just sounded like desperate pleading, which it was.

"Stop lying, Elizabeth," my mom broke in, and I could tell she was even angrier than she had been last night. I had hoped she would have calmed down some, but she had obviously brewed over it all night. "Are you forgetting I could smell the beer on your breath last night and that you admitted you had been drinking? That's the trouble with lying. You can't remember what lies you told. Start telling the truth, and you won't have to worry about contradicting yourself." She was definitely raising her voice, and her neck and cheeks were deep red, almost purple.

Before I could respond, my dad came back at me. "Elizabeth, I'm with your mom on this. This quarterback boy is obviously a bad influence on you. Before you started seeing him, you didn't drink or smoke pot, and you were honest with us. Honestly, we don't even recognize you right now," he finished.

I started to respond because now I was just as angry as they were, but my dad cut me off.

"Don't speak. Just listen," he said. As he said this, I knew right away there would be no talking my way out of this. I should have seen it in their expressions when I first came into the kitchen, but I had held out hope for impartiality while I pleaded my case, hoping to win over my dad with logic since he had always been so level-headed. Now, I realized it was too late. It had gone too far. My mom had jumped to conclusions, and of course, my dad supported her. It still stung, and as he continued speaking, I began to get so angry that although I heard the words, I couldn't process them.

Only later, after I stormed out of the kitchen and back up to my room and eventually calmed down, did it begin to sink in what he had said…what my punishment--the prison sentence--they had imposed.

For the next two weeks, my mom would drive me to school and pick me up. I would be dropped off right before school began and picked up right after school ended.

I would be confined to my room for the original week my mom had imposed, plus an additional week for trying to argue with them that morning and the previous night, even though I hadn't argued at all. During the two weeks, they said I was not to see Blake and that my punishment would be extended if they learned I had broken their sanctions.

Indignation and outrage burned in my stomach all afternoon as I stayed in my room. I had skipped breakfast, and at noon, when my mom said I could come down to get something to eat, I lied and said I wasn't hungry. By dinner, I was ravenous, but when I came down to eat, I fixed myself a peanut butter and apricot jam sandwich and took it back to my room to eat instead of eating the baked spaghetti casserole my mom had cooked--even though it was my favorite.

At 8 o'clock, I decided to risk checking my phone to text Blake and Rebecca so I could let them know what was going on. My parents hadn't said anything about not using my phone and hadn't even said anything about not texting Blake, only that I was forbidden to see him. I knew I was splitting hairs and that if I was caught, I would certainly get into more trouble, but I decided I had to risk it.

I decided to wait and tell Rebecca in person. I didn't want to be on my phone any longer than possible, and my priority was Blake since he would be the most affected if I followed my parent's directive. I decided to text him so that there would be less chance of my parents finding out by overhearing and taking my phone away. I kept it short and to the point. "Last night was great. I'm grounded for 2 weeks. Might not see you. Sorry." I looked at it for a couple of seconds before hitting send. I was getting more and more depressed as it sank in that I might not see Blake for two weeks.

As I waited for a reply, I thought about how much had changed recently. A few weeks ago, the biggest punishment would have been not being able to go to the library for a couple of weeks. Now, I had this person in my life I never expected. My life had seemed so full before, but looking back, I realized how empty it had been. I had been hiding in the library, behind books, not building any relationships or opening myself up to anyone. I had Rebecca, but even with her, I hadn't really opened up. I hadn't been able to talk to her about my fears, hopes, or anything beyond test scores and homework. Blake had rescued me from all of that. I was going to miss him, but I felt even worse for him. He had told me how alone he had felt before we met. I felt guilty knowing that he would probably miss me, but I also felt glad that I had someone who would miss me. It was funny that I knew it was only going to be two weeks, but now those two weeks felt like forever. Without even talking to Blake, I knew he would feel the same. We'd only had two dates and spent a few lunch periods together, but I knew that I wouldn't be able to go back to the kind of life I had just a few weeks before. A life filled with books, tests, and studying and nothing else. Now I had someone I could really talk to, open up. He had opened up to me, and I felt like I knew him better than anyone, and as odd as it seemed, I thought he knew me better than anyone else--even my parents.

I got his text just a few minutes later. "So much 4 understanding parents. Lol. understand, but will be difficult 2 not cu. Last night was worth it. Maybe we can still meet at lunch.. Will miss you, but remember, only for 2 weeks."

I reread his text a couple of times before shutting off my phone. I decided not to risk texting him back in case my mom came into my room and saw me with my phone. I didn't want to give her any reason to extend my punishment to three weeks.

I lay on my comforter, staring at the ceiling. I knew I had homework and studying to do, but I couldn't bring myself to start. I kept thinking about the night before. Blake had kissed me and then said he was falling for me. I had never dated anyone before, but I knew my feelings for him were strong. I cared more for him than anything else in my life right now. I wondered, was I being just a silly school girl? My room grew dark as it became later, and my thoughts continued their inner preoccupation. My indignation and anger were spent, and all I felt was the loss of the time I would not be spending with Blake. At some point, I drifted off to sleep.

The next morning was Sunday, and I decided to approach things with a different tactic. I woke up early, got dressed, and went downstairs to make my mom and dad breakfast. Even though it was barely 6 o'clock, I came into the kitchen and found both of my parents already sitting at the table, my dad drinking his coffee with a lot of cream and sugar like he always did, and my mom drinking her orange blossom tea.

They both looked up when I entered, and even though neither of them smiled, I could tell a lot of the vexation from the previous day had dissipated. I could have another try at changing their minds now that their moods had softened, but I decided not to try to nettle them anymore and to stick with my plan of being their *sweet little daughter*. I would convince them that I had not changed into a moody, disobedient teenager on a drinking and drug binge--so ridiculous for them to even think that--and that Blake had been a good influence on me. Maybe when my grounding was over, I would even invite Blake over for dinner so that they could see how he really was, how sweet and caring he was--not at all like the picture they had painted the day before.

"Good morning," I chirped. "I was thinking about making some eggs or waffles. Do either of you want me to make you some, or anything else," I said with as much eagerness and delight as I could manage.

"None for me, thanks," replied my dad.

"I'll pass too, hun," my mom said, "but thanks for the offer." She looked over at my dad, who returned the look as if they were conveying some Soviet secrets during the Cold War. My mom obviously knew what I was trying to do, but I decided to just stay the course and stay with the same approach whether or not it yielded fruitful results. As long as I remained pleasant and acted the part, there was no way they could extend my punishment, I reasoned. And then, in just two short weeks, I could start going out with Blake again.

I ended up just having a bowl of raisin bran mixed with Frosted Flakes. I was really starting to like the mixture. The yellow box of Cheerios sat unopened on the pantry shelf. After I put my dishes in the dishwasher, I went back to my room since the terms of my incarceration were that I was to be confined there when not eating, using the restroom, or going to school. I read through my notes for my government and science classes, emailing a copy to Rebecca before completing my calculus homework and then finishing my composition for Creative Writing, which I decided to do on how teens are assumed guilty by parents who are in a rush to judgment.

I finished all my work before noon and went downstairs for a quick lunch. My mom was vacuuming the den, and my dad was in his office, so neither of them even heard me come downstairs. I made myself a peanut butter and jelly sandwich with apricot jam and added a little honey to the side with the peanut butter. I quickly ate it in my room at my desk and wondered what I should do the rest of the day, really the rest of the week, since I wouldn't be able to go to the library.

My thoughts drifted to Blake, naturally. I would miss him, but in a way, he was being punished too. I knew how alone he had felt before we had met because he had told me he had nobody to talk to or hang out with. He had said over and over how alone and depressed he had been after his mom had left him. He had his dad, and he had football, but he had said he avoided his dad as much as possible. He enjoyed football but had called all the people in his life shallow and hollow shells devoid of personality. It had been the harshest thing I had heard him say, with the exception of how he described his dad. All these thoughts added to my gloom, and I started wondering if there was something I could do to cheer him up until my punishment was over.

I started thinking about his mom. He obviously loved his mom and spoke affectionately about her. They had obviously gotten along well and had a great relationship, so I wondered what had happened to make her run off and leave him. I was sure she had her reasons for leaving, but I couldn't fathom why she hadn't taken Blake with her. It sounded like she had loved him very much. Was this just how Blake had seen her? Maybe she wasn't as benevolent as Blake had described her, but was like many people--more self-centered and self-absorbed--putting her needs above everything and everyone else, even her son. Blake had made it sound like his dad was pretty abusive, so I tried not to be too harsh in my judgment, but I just couldn't make myself objective. I thought of the little boy Blake I had met on the bus. He was so vulnerable. Even back then, he had a smile that was difficult to forget. Somehow, Blake's mom had forgotten his smile, forgotten him, and abandoned him. Left him.

Out of the blue, it came to me. Blake had said she had gone. She had left him. I knew that Blake still had very raw feelings about that. He tried to hide it, but when he talked about her--even just mentioning her--a deep pain crossed his eyes. I decided I could do something for Blake.

I decided that I would do what I could to try to find her. I would find Blake's mom for him.

When I got back to my room with my sandwich, I started thinking about how to accomplish the task--my gift to Blake. A person could find most things using the internet these days, but I didn't even know her name or Blake's dad's name. I only knew their last name was Patterson. I was technically forbidden from talking to or seeing Blake, and I didn't know if I would even see him at school or not. Even seeing him at school ran a risk because my parents had said if they learned I had seen him, my punishment would be extended. Even if I did see him, I couldn't just come out and ask what his mom's name was. That would raise suspicion, and I wanted it to be a surprise.

I lay in bed thinking about my dilemma for an hour before I finally decided I would have to enlist Rebecca's help. I lay in bed another hour, considering whether to call or text Rebecca or wait until Monday. After a long argument with myself, I decided to wait until Monday morning. Once I decided that there was not much else to do so, I spent the rest of the day trying to figure out how to help Rebecca ferret out the information without Blake figuring out what she was up to. Blake could read people very easily, but Rebecca was a bit hard to figure out anyway. Sunday passed, and Monday quickly approached.

Chapter 7
Secret Mission

On Monday morning, I was up and ready by 6:30 even though school didn't start until 8:05. I had hoped if I was ready early that, my mom would relent or forget and just drop me off at school early. She was sitting at the kitchen table, drinking coffee and doing a crossword puzzle.

"Good morning, Mom," I chirped. "I'm ready to go whenever you are."

She didn't even raise her eyes from her crossword puzzle but I could see the corners of her mouth twitch up a fraction in a miniscule smile. "Nice try, Elizabeth, but you and I both know school doesn't start until around 8, so we will be leaving at 7:45. Are you going to eat breakfast?"

I sighed heavily and headed for the pantry cabinet to pull out the Frosted Flakes and raisin bran. I was rinsing my bowl when my phone buzzed. I looked over at my mom. She had clearly heard it but was pretending she didn't. Clearly, she was waiting to see what I would do. I checked my phone to see who it was. "Mom, that's Rebecca wondering where I am. We usually study in the morning before school. Do you mind if I text her back that I won't make it?"

"Of course, Elizabeth. We didn't say you couldn't message Rebecca about school," she replied. For some reason, her response annoyed me. I felt like she was being petty and had blown everything out of proportion. I took a deep breath to calm myself so that I didn't get myself into more trouble. I had always been so calm and, collected and rational, but lately, my emotions had become unpredictable and erratic. On the other hand, was it really my fault that my parents had started acting so capriciously? It really riled me that they had suddenly started treating me like a child. Had all these years of my behaving and all their years of supposed open-mindedness been an act? Maybe they were waiting all along for me to fail so they could pounce.

I was thinking myself into a very cross mood, and I knew that was a bad idea, so I decided to completely change my routine to take my mind off things. I put my bowl back on the table and went back to the pantry, taking out the package of Oreos. I filled the bowl with Oreos, poured milk over them, and started in on my second breakfast. If nothing else, this seemed to dumbfound my mom, who stopped working on her crossword puzzle and just stared at me. I could tell she wanted to say something but couldn't think of anything to say. I hadn't broken any rules. She was treating me like a child, so I would do something childish. I texted Rebecca back about the situation I was in, told her I would explain more during lunch, and kept eating my milk-soaked Oreos.

By the end of the bowl, my mood had partially improved because of the sugar high. I went back upstairs, brushed my teeth, and came back to the table to read through a chapter in my Calculus book until it was time to go. When my mom announced that it was time to go, I was so engrossed in a problem that it startled me out of a deep concentration.

When we got into my mom's silver Honda, I was careful not to slam the door. I wanted to do everything I could to play the part of the obedient, repentant daughter, thinking it never hurt to show contrition. There was always a chance my punishment would be lifted before the two weeks for good behavior--as unlikely as that seemed at this time.

I had hoped that we would arrive at school at least a few minutes early, but my mom drove like a sloth in a snowstorm, so when she pulled up, the bell for the first period was already ringing, so I had to hurry. I was actually glad people were already heading to classes so that fewer of them saw me being dropped off by my mom like a freshman on the first day of school. I said a quick goodbye and rushed to my history/government class, which was in the building next to the library.

I sighed as I walked up the steps and looked back at the library. I already missed my time before school there. It wasn't that I needed the time to study, but more that I used the time to destress, and honestly, I had used the time to avoid interacting with people. Now that I had a relationship with Blake, I didn't really need to avoid people--to worry about rejection and being made fun of as the nerd of the group--except that for the next two weeks, I was "prohibited" from seeing Blake. I was sure that I could find a way around that, and I looked forward to lunch when I could complain to Rebecca about how unfair my parents were being, and I could hopefully see Blake. It had only been a couple of days, but already it felt like ages since I had seen Blake. As I sat in history/government class, my mind kept wandering back to the kiss and to Blake, telling me he thought he was falling for me. My parents couldn't take that away from me, no matter what they tried.

By lunch, I could hardly stand it. It seemed bizarre to me that just a few weeks previous, I had preferred solitude and loved my time by myself, but now I couldn't wait to talk to Rebecca and Blake. I had gone from being indifferent to people to feeling isolated and deserted. So much had changed since I had met Blake. My life felt more full, and I felt like I was on a different path. I was still interested in school, books, academics, and tests, but I wasn't consumed by them anymore. Now, my life was fuller. I had always had Rebecca as a friend, but I had always taken her for granted. I had not really valued our friendship. I was just as happy to hang out alone in the library without her--or anybody. Now, I felt deserted being alone all morning, and I craved company. I was happy keeping my thoughts and feelings bottled up before, but now I had to tell someone. I felt like I would burst. Blake had brought up so many emotions that I hadn't even known I had. I thought back to our last night together. I was definitely falling for him, too.

Lunch finally came, and I quickly walked to the Quad to meet Rebecca. I spotted her on the grass holding a large sack, a huge backpack slung over her shoulders, looking around like she was lost. No wonder she stood out, I thought. It looked like she had every single book in the whole school in her backpack. I walked up to within three feet of her before she spotted me, even though she had been obviously looking for me.

A look of relief washed over her face when she spotted me. "Hi, Elizabeth. So, what happened?" she burst out the second she spotted me.

I wanted to tell her, but there was something I wanted more. "Where's Blake? I thought he would be here," I replied.

"He said he didn't want to do anything to get you into more trouble and that he's going to respect your parents' rules."

I knew I was overreacting, but I felt like my stomach had bounced around and ended up in my throat, making it difficult to speak. All morning, I had looked forward to seeing Blake, prohibition or not. I don't know if I was angry at my parents, Blake or Rebecca, but my mood instantly soured. We found a bench and sat under a tree, and I poured out to Rebecca what had happened as she ate her sandwich, chips, pudding, cookies, and drank her juice. By the time she was done, I was almost hoarse. I hadn't talked long, but the emotion of it all had drained me more than I expected. Rebecca just listened while I complained and talked. I didn't tell her about the kiss or about what Blake had said. Some things were too private still, but as I talked to Rebecca, I felt a little better. I had never talked to her about anything personal before. She had always been open with me, talking about her dad and mom, vampires, boys she thought were cute, and anything she thought, but I had always kept my part of the conversations about school and homework. It had taken Blake to make me realize how lonely I had been. I had been isolated without even realizing it. My emotions had always been remote and hidden, but now I poured out everything to Rebecca, and she took it in like a true friend would.

By the end of lunch, I felt better. I was tired from the emotions I had pushed out, and I had skipped lunch, not feeling like I could keep anything down if I tried, but I still felt better. The one thing Rebecca kept repeating was, "Well, at least it's only for two weeks. It'll be over before you know it." I knew that was true, and it helped hearing it over and over, but it still felt like a lifetime.

I told Rebecca she would have to talk to Blake and somehow find out his mom's name without letting him know why.

"That part will be easy since I don't know why, myself," she said.

"I just want to surprise him with something to make up for not seeing him or being at the games the next two weeks," I explained, knowing it didn't really explain anything.

One good thing about Rebecca was that she was always very agreeable and conceded without asking too many questions. We said our goodbyes and headed back to class. I would be picked up right after school, so Rebecca said she would look for Blake then, before football practice began, and would try to casually bring up his mom to find out information.

After school, my mom was parked right in front of the Quad. I had hoped she would be late, but I knew that hope was unrealistic because she was always punctual, and she would be especially punctual to prove her point and make sure I adhered to my punishment. She smiled big when I opened the door and got into the silver Honda and said, "How was your day?" as if she always picked me up from school and we were the best of friends.

"Fine," I replied, determined not to speak too much on the way home. She took the hint and pulled away from the curb without commenting any further. On the ride home, she made occasional comments about insignificant things she noticed as we drove along.

I kept sullen and quiet for the most part and only gave a "Mmm hmm," every so often. I tried to be civil, but I couldn't force myself to pretend everything was peachy and that I was happy about the situation. I kept racking my brain, trying to figure out how to get out of this, but my mom had just as big of a brain as I had, and I could see that she had thought of everything and had left no loopholes. I would just have to endure the two weeks. At least I had something to focus on, I thought to myself. Blake would be so happy if I was able to find his mom. From what little he had said, it had sounded like she had left because of abuse from Blake's dad. She had not wanted to leave Blake but had no choice. I was certain she would be overjoyed to find out he was okay and doing so well. I was determined to do this for him.

The rest of the week dragged on. I was dropped off right before the bell rang for first period. I had lunch with Rebecca, and I missed Blake more and more. I began to worry about not seeing Blake. What if he realized he didn't like me as much as he thought he had? What if he found someone else? Rebecca laughed when I mentioned my worries to her. She had been seeing him every morning before school but so far had not been able to find out anything about his mom.

By Thursday, I was becoming desperate. "Rebecca, you need to try harder. I need to find out what his mom's name is so I can proceed with my surprise for him." I know I sounded frenzied, but the longer the time stretched without seeing Blake, the less I cared about appearing demoralized.

"I've tried, Elizabeth. It's not easy because you told me I had to ask without him knowing anything. I don't even know myself! How do you ask someone a question without asking them a question?" she replied, exasperated.

"I don't know," I said. "Just keep trying," I pleaded.

On Thursday, I got a little snippy at Rebecca. It was lunchtime, and I had assumed that since I wasn't able to go to the game, that she would stay home too. While I felt slightly hysterical, Rebecca seemed her usual happy self. This annoyed me to no end. How could she be happy when I was so gloomy? Finally, I asked her, "You're not going to the game tomorrow, are you?"

She didn't even have the decency to pause before answering, "Sure I am. I always go to the game."

I took a deep breath to keep myself from exploding. "How can you go when I can't?" I demanded.

"I've always gone, even before you started coming," she replied as if that explained everything.

"Are you going out with Blake after the game," I demanded.

Rebecca stopped and looked at me as if just noticing my mood. "Um, no. Why would I go out with Blake? He's your boyfriend. He'll probably go to some party that the popular kids go to, and I'll go home like I always do. What's with you, Elizabeth?"

I grabbed a handful of Cheese-its and shoved them in my mouth to give myself a minute before answering.

"Sorry, Rebecca. I'm just really stressed out." I knew she didn't deserve to be mistreated by me. She hadn't done anything wrong. I tried to soften my mood, but I was already pretty wound up. Then I said something without thinking that I immediately wished I could take back. "You just don't know what it's like to have a boyfriend."

I could tell by the redness in her cheeks that my remark had stung. I hadn't meant it to be an insult, but how else could she take it?

Rebecca turned away from me so I could not see her face. She murmured, "Well, I have to get to class. I'll see you tomorrow."

Rebecca and I had been friends for as long as I could remember, but I had always taken her for granted. I had always made her play by my rules; always put me first. As she walked away, I felt the shame of how thoughtless, selfish, and insensitive I had been.

CHAPTER 8
YOUR DUMB FRIEND,

I spent the night trying to figure out how everything had gotten so disordered. My relationship with my parents, my best friend, and even my boyfriend--it took me a minute to even comprehend this new relationship that just a few weeks previous had seemed impossible--were spiraling out of control.

My parents didn't trust me. I had always been their dependable, reliable, and stable little girl. Now, they viewed me as some hormonal teenager who partied and snuck around. Rebecca had always been so trustworthy and faithful, and I had betrayed her trust. All she wanted was friendship and to fit in, and I had pointed out how out of place she was, how different she was. Neither of us had ever had a boyfriend, so we had been on equal footing, but now that I had one, I had pointed to the fact that she had never had a relationship and, therefore, couldn't understand. Even if it was partially true, the meanness of what I had done still shamed me. I had hurt her without thinking. I began to wonder if I ever really thought about anyone else. Maybe I was so caught up in being the perfect student and daughter that I had started to believe I was better than others. While it was true that Rebecca didn't really fit in, when I looked at myself, I was pretty much in the same boat as she. At the party Blake had taken me to, I had felt out of place and didn't really relate to anyone-- except maybe Perla, who for some reason, I felt an immediate connection with.

My relationship with Blake still surprised me because I really didn't know what he saw in me. There were so many girls far prettier than I was. I was book smart, but Blake really understood people and had a wisdom and understanding I couldn't get from books. I hadn't spoken to him for a week now. I hadn't even dared to text him again in case my mom asked to see my phone. I had to make it up to him and to Rebecca. I just knew that if I could help find his mom, it would make a lot of things better.

For Rebecca, I decided I needed to start trusting her, so the next morning, I decided to tell her my plan to find Blake's mom. Even though my mom had not said I couldn't text or call, I still was worried about her asking to see my phone to see what I was up to. If she somehow decided I hadn't abided by the rules she had set out, I didn't want to give her any excuse to extend my punishment. I decided to send Rebecca an email and then a text telling her to read the email I sent.

I thought about what to write while I ate breakfast. My mom was working a crossword puzzle at the table, pretending not to watch me, but every once in a while, she would sneak a quick glance at me, and I could tell she was wondering what I was up to. When I got back to my room, I opened up my laptop and started typing:

Rebecca,

I am so sorry about yesterday. I hope you can forgive me for not thinking before talking. I know I haven't been a good friend lately, and I'm going to work on that. I hope you know how much I value our friendship.

I'm working on trying to find Blake's mom to surprise him. He really misses her and I want to do something for him. All I know is that he said she left around his freshman year. I would love to tell him where she is so he can go and see her. I can explain more when I see you. Sorry again for yesterday.

Your dumb friend,

When I finished the email, I looked it over, made a couple of quick changes, and hit send. Then I grabbed my phone, texted Rebecca to read the email I just sent, and then deleted the text I sent to her. I didn't want any evidence, just in case. After this, I lay back in bed to think things through and fell back asleep.

I woke up after one and was hungry since I hadn't eaten lunch, so I went downstairs to the kitchen. My mom was still at the table, but now she was reading a book. My dad was nowhere to be seen, so I figured he went into the office to catch up on some work. I made myself a peanut butter and apricot/pineapple jam sandwich and grabbed a box of Cheez-Its. I was halfway through my sandwich when my mom looked up and innocently said, "Elizabeth, can I see your phone?"

I dug it out of my pocket, unlocked it, and handed it over, thinking that I had been right to be cautious. "Sure, Mom," I said as nonchalantly as I could.

She scrolled through my texts before giving it back. "Just checking to make sure you are abiding by the terms of your grounding and not texting that quarterback boy of yours," she said, handing it back to me.

"Of course, Mom. Anything you want," I said as innocently as I could. Her eyes narrowed, and I thought she had figured it out and would ask for the phone back to check again. I smiled just a little, realizing she could check all she wanted and wouldn't find anything. I tried to keep my face expressionless as I took another bite of my sandwich and reached into the Cheez-Its box. She continued to watch me eat, and we both sat in silence, probably thinking the same thing.

The rest of the weekend I spent in my room studying. My mind seemed clearer, and the studying helped me focus even more. It also seemed to calm me down the rest of the way so that by Monday morning, when my mom drove me to school, I was actually in a good mood. I could tell this made my mom even more suspicious, but I didn't care. I was halfway through my grounding, and on Friday, I would be able to see Blake again.

I didn't see Rebecca before the bell rang for the first period, but at lunch, we met for lunch outside the library. She was beaming when I walked up to her, and I could tell all was forgiven. I decided I should apologize again in person just to make it official.

"Hi, Rebecca. Listen, I wanted to say again how sorry…"

She interrupted me, "Oh that, don't worry about it. Guess what?" she blurted out immediately, and I could tell she was excited.

I thought for a second and couldn't think of anything that would get her excited. "You got the results back from Friday's chemistry test?" I guessed.

She didn't wait an instant before answering, "Not even close, but I did talk to Blake this morning." Her expression was a mix of excitement and eagerness, as if she had just scored higher on a test than I had--something that had only occurred three times in our past. She paused like she wanted to drag it out and keep me guessing but couldn't wait to blurt it out.

"And?" I said after she didn't say anything else.

"And I know the name of Blake's mom," she declared.

Now, I was caught up in excitement. "What? How?"

"Well," Rebecca began, "once you trusted me with the information I needed in order to perform the task, I formulated a plan and executed it flawlessly." She seemed very proud of herself, but to be honest, it was well deserved, and I would have told her so if I hadn't been dying to know the details.

"Come on, out with it," I urged. "Tell me everything."

"I figured after what you told me that Blake's mom must have been coming to all the games his freshman year. So, this morning, I was talking to Blake, and I flat out said to him, 'I think I remember your mom used to come to some of the games. Wasn't she the lady with the dark, curly hair like yours?' I asked. I just made that part up," she explained.

I gestured for her to continue, and she said, "So I said, 'Her name was Martha, right?' I picked a name that starts with an *M* because that's the most common letter for women's names in English."

I had to hand it to her. Rebecca was brilliant. Sometimes, I forgot how smart she really was because I had been so focused on myself--something I again vowed to change.

"So he got this weird look, and at first I thought he was suspicious, but then he just said, 'No, her name was Connie…Connie Ray.'" Rebecca paused for a moment as if waiting for an audience to applaud.

"Wow!" I said as if on cue. "You're such a brainiac. I would not have thought of doing something like that. Well played."

She beamed even more for a minute before turning somber. "I kind of felt bad about it, though," she said. "He looked miserable for a bit right after I brought her up."

I felt a little dispirited knowing that I had caused Blake to think about something painful, but I told myself it was only temporary because once I found his mom, he would be able to talk to her and would be overjoyed at being reunited with her. I knew he blamed himself for her leaving him even though it had nothing to do with him. He had once told me that he hadn't done enough to help her, to keep her here--that he had been too focused on himself, much like I realized I had been too focused on myself to appreciate Rebecca and, if I had to admit it, even my parents. I told Rebecca that it was all for the greater good and that I hoped soon to have something that would cheer him back up.

She brightened again and started talking about the lunar eclipse that would be coming up in seven days. She called it a blood moon and said it only happens about three times a year and would be in the perfect position in the sky to observe it and how it wouldn't be this perfect again for three years. I paid attention and tried to sound interested since I was determined to be a better friend to Rebecca. I knew she didn't normally like being out after dark by herself. She tried to pass it off as fear of vampires, but I think she was really just afraid of the dark. The blood moon was supposed to occur at 10:21 on the next Friday, one week from today and Rebecca said she was glad my grounding would be over by then so that I could be with her and she wouldn't have to worry about being alone because vampires only strike people when they are by themselves. I almost laughed when she said this because I knew she would somehow bring up vampires. I held it together, though, and told her I would be glad to go with her to observe the eclipse.

We talked about where we should go to watch it, and I realized then that it was right after the game. I hadn't seen Blake in almost a week now and my first day of freedom would be Friday. I had planned on going to the game and then going out with Blake afterward. That was assuming Blake still wanted to see me. I tried to push my doubts away. It had been less than a week, I told myself. I thought back to the last time I had seen him. He had said he was falling for me. We had kissed--not just a brush on the cheek, but a real kiss. I suddenly missed the smell of his earthy, woody scent.

I tried to think about what to do. I had just said I would be there for Rebecca and had pledged to myself to be a better friend to her--especially after she had come through for me--but I hadn't seen Blake in a week. I couldn't ask him to wait longer. I couldn't wait any longer. I had to see him that night, but I couldn't disappoint Rebecca. This blood moon thing sounded like a big deal to her. I would have to find some way to work it all out.

The bell rang, and we headed to our classes, neither of us having eaten lunch. I had a week to come up with a solution, and my mind was already working through the problem. I knew I would think of something.

That Saturday morning, I had time to start my research on Blake's mom, Connie Ray Patterson. I got up early and went downstairs to have breakfast so I could work uninterrupted from after breakfast until lunch. When I got downstairs, my mom was at the table as usual. Even though it was early Saturday morning, she was dressed as if she were ready to go into an office or courtroom in a navy blue skirt and white button-up top. The only thing that indicated she wasn't headed to work was that instead of the high heels she used to wear to work, she wore furry slippers. I was barefoot and wish I had thought to wear slippers. The cold kitchen floor tile sent a shiver right up through my feet all the way throughout my whole body. I also wished I had thrown on a robe over my thin pajamas. I decided it was probably time to switch from my short summer pajamas to my warmer winter pajamas.

I looked in the cupboard to see what I wanted. Today, I decided to go back to my Cheerios. As I grabbed a bowl and poured the milk, I noticed my mom watching me while trying to look like she was looking at her crossword book. I decided to be cordial so that I could continue to present the all-is-fine-and-returned-to-normal appearance.

"Good morning, Mom," I said as cheerfully as I could.

She looked at me before smiling back. "Good morning, Elizabeth. What are your plans today?"

"Nothing much," I replied. "Just doing research." She eyed me suspiciously as if she knew something was up, but I was doing research after all. I just wasn't doing schoolwork like I usually did every Saturday. Somehow, she could always tell when something was different.

I ate my breakfast, rinsed my bowl, and headed back upstairs. While I brushed my teeth and changed, I thought about how I would track down Blake's mom. I decided I would start with a general Google search and then maybe look up online records from the county courthouse. After a week of feeling miserable and persecuted, I was finally feeling better. In a week's time, things would begin to return to normal, I would be able to start seeing Blake again, and I would have exciting news for him. I sat at my desk and started typing on my laptop. I typed Blake's mom's name in and hit return. I didn't expect to hit paydirt right away. There were actually quite a few Connie Ray Pattersons in the United States. There were a lot of social media sites that listed variations of her name. I repeated the search with variations of her name, including Constance and Rae, and got the same results. I filtered through them over the next couple of hours, hoping to come across one that might be her, but of the many results, none matched up with what I thought was her. Most were out of state and the wrong age. I worked through the leads, eliminating them one by one and adding more criteria that might bring her up in my search.

By lunchtime, I was beginning to become discouraged. I decided to make a quick sandwich and think about different strategies while I took a break. My mom was still at the table but had switched to sneakers and was reading a book when I went down.

She looked up as I entered the kitchen. "How's the research?" she asked politely.

"Um, it's okay. It's harder than I thought it would be, but I'll get it done," I replied with equal politeness and honesty.

"What class is it for?" she asked. "Maybe I can help."

I froze like a statue in the middle of spreading peanut butter on a slice of bread. She had never asked to help me with research before. Of course, I had never complained about it being difficult. I wondered if she knew something or if I was just imagining things.

"That's okay," I returned. "I just have to put the time in. You know how it is."

"Okay, well you know I'm here if you need me," she responded. She sounded genuine. Perhaps she was trying to mend fences by offering to help. I decided to assume the best and not drive myself crazy with suspicious conspiracies.

I took my sandwich and Cheez-Its upstairs and took a bite before setting the plate down on my desk next to my laptop. As I ate, I decided to narrow my search to something more local. It was likely that she had stayed in the city, so searching the online archives of the local newspapers might yield something. If she had stayed in the city, there had to be some record of her.

I went into the searchable online newspaper database (SOND) website that our local newspaper used to archive past articles. All previous articles dating back ten years or so were stored on their database, and a person could look up anything published in the paper, provided it was after the newspaper went digital. If it was published before then, a person would have to go to the library and look up copies of the newspaper on microfiche.

I created a free account, clicked on the local news tab, and entered the name Connie Ray Patterson. The results came back quickly and showed no exact matches. There were quite a few stories with the name Patterson, but I wanted to try to narrow it down so I wouldn't be spending all afternoon on a wild goose chase.

I tried again with Constance Ray Patterson. I hit enter, and instantly, two stories popped up. One was a news story, and the other was an obituary. I swallowed hard as I moved the mouse over to the obituary story, hoping it was a different person. Connie could be short for Constance so that was why I had tried a search under that name. Now, I hesitated. What if I found Blake's mom, but it was too late? What if she had died, and there could be no reconciliation? If I found that out, should I keep it to myself or tell Blake and let him deal with it. I felt like somehow not knowing would be worse, but then he had already experienced so much pain; I didn't know if I could bring more pain into his life.

I took a deep breath and clicked on the story:

Constance Ray Patterson, 33, died on Friday night. No memorial service is planned at this time. She is survived by her husband, Jessie Patterson, and her 15-year-old son, Blake Patterson...

I stopped reading. After a minute--or an hour--I let out the breath I hadn't realized I had been holding. I rapidly blinked my eyes repeatedly to try to focus them. For some reason, they were blurry. I reached up to rub them and realized my cheeks were wet. I didn't know what to do next. I had found Blake's mom.

Chapter 9
Miss Four-Point-0

I stared at the screen for several minutes that seemed to stretch into hours. I kept going back and forth. I have to tell Blake. How can I tell Blake? But I have to tell him…how can I not? Finally, I shut the screen of my laptop. I felt so bad for Blake, for the pain I knew he would feel when I told him…because I knew I had to. I wouldn't want something like this kept from me, no matter how painful it might be. I knew he would be upset, but I knew he would be more upset if I didn't tell him. I just had to figure out how and when. I racked my brain, going over different scenarios, trying to figure out the best way to break the news to him.

After some time, I noticed my room had dimmed considerably and that I was sitting in near dark. I looked over at the clock on my nightstand. It was already 6 o'clock. I wasn't hungry, but I couldn't stay in my room any longer. I went downstairs into the kitchen, where my mom and dad were already eating.

"There she is," my dad said when I walked in.

My mom only looked at me. "Elizabeth, is everything alright?" Somehow, she knew that something was wrong.

"Yeah, I'm just tired from studying all day?" I lied. Of course, I couldn't tell them why I was upset. I put some food on my plate and managed a few bites without really tasting any of it. I was like a robot, eating on remote control, going through motions without paying attention to anything I was doing.

After dinner, I went back to my room and eventually fell asleep in my bed, still in my clothes.

I don't even remember the rest of the weekend, but I woke up on Monday with a sense of dread. I had decided I would tell Blake today. I would skip my seventh period class, study hall-- because it was the easiest class to skip-- and wait outside the Social Studies building where Blake had history/government.

My mom looked up when I came into the kitchen late. "I was beginning to wonder if you were coming down," she said with a worried look on her face. It's almost time to go."

"I know. I'm sorry," I apologized. "I overslept." I hadn't really slept much at all, but I had stayed in bed until I absolutely had to get up.

"Why don't you grab something to eat on the way?" she suggested.

"Actually, I'm not even hungry," I answered truthfully.

As she drove me to school, she kept stealing worried glances at me. When we got to school, she wished me a good day, and I said thanks and, got out of the car and went to my first period. All day long, I was in a daze. During lunch, I met Rebecca. She asked if I found out anything about Blake's mom, but I told her I was still researching. I couldn't tell her anything before talking to Blake.

The day pressed on, and I went to all of my classes, but my mind was somewhere else. I kept trying to think of reasons not to tell him. How can I cause someone I care so much about so much pain? I asked myself. I kept coming back to the decision I had made the first night. He has to know. He has to be able to put it to rest.

After lunch, I went to science class with Ms. Hart. I didn't even take notes, even though I knew there would likely be a test the next day. She liked to spring "surprise" quizzes on Mondays. My sixth-period class was creative writing, but I don't remember what, if anything, I wrote about.

When the bell rang, I darted out of the classroom and pushed my way through the crowds to make my way outside and over to the Social Studies building. I waited at the steps as students pushed by. After just a couple of minutes, I saw Blake walking toward me. He had no backpack or books and was almost to the steps before he saw me. He looked confused for a moment and then smiled.

"Is your grounding over early? It's so good to see you," he replied. I was instantly torn between wanting to just hug him and pretend that everything was okay and knowing that I had to give him news that would change his life and could possibly change our relationship.

"Can we talk for a minute?" I asked. He grabbed my hand, and we walked around the corner of the building. The bell rang, and we were both officially tardy, but neither of us seemed to care. He smiled his crooked smile at me, grabbed my other hand, and waited.

I took a deep breath to begin but then waited. I wanted to tell him, but I still struggled with knowing it would cause him pain. Finally, I let out my breath slowly, took another deep breath, and began.

"Blake, I have to tell you something," I began. He looked at me, waiting for me to continue. "It's about your mom," I continued.

Suddenly, his smile left his face, and his expression turned darker. "What about her?" he asked.

"Well, I know you said she left you and your dad..." I stammered. This was even harder than I thought it would be. "So, I thought maybe you would like to know where she went so...you know...you could contact her if you wanted to..." I paused for a moment. Blake's face looked confused. I decided the best way was just to continue. "So I did some research to try to find out where she went and what happened to her…"

"Why would you do that!" he suddenly demanded. I was caught off guard by his rise in volume. "I told you," he continued, "She's gone. You didn't need to look into anything. It wasn't any of your business!" He was nearly shouting, and I didn't know what to do. His expression scared me.

I supposed he was still hurt, thinking she had abandoned him. I had to just blurt it out. "Blake, I found her obituary. I'm sorry…she died. I know it hurts, but I thought…" So much pain crossed his face that I wanted to take it back.

"Blake…" That was as far as I got. Blake cut me off angrily. "Why did you think it was any of your business?!" he shouted. "Just because you're smart doesn't give you the right to poke your nose into everything!" as he said this, his eyes took on a rage that I had never seen before.

I took a step back. "I'm sorry," I began. "I just thought I could help…"

"Well, you can't solve everything, even if you are Miss Four-Point-O," he said angrily. I could tell he was hurt, but I couldn't understand what was happening. I was hurt and confused. I never thought he would react like this. I knew he would be sad and hurt, but I had no idea why he was angry.

"I'm sorry," I tried again. "I was just trying to help."

"I need some time alone," he said angrily. His watery eyes looked like they held deep pain and anger. I had no idea why he was reacting this way.

He started walking away, and before he was out of sight, he was running. I was completely dumbfounded by what had just happened.

I wandered to the front of the school to wait for my mom to pick me up. I sat on a rock planter in front of the school between two trees, trying to wrap my head around what had just happened. Not only was Blake's reaction unexpected, it just didn't make sense at all. I wiped my eyes so that my mom wouldn't see that I'd been crying. I pulled out my phone, thinking maybe I should call or text Blake, but I couldn't think of anything to say that would help. Besides, I had already tried to help and I'd just made a mess of everything.

My mind kept going in a circle, replaying the events of the last hour. In the distance, I heard a car horn. After a few seconds, I heard it again, blaring longer. I looked up and my mom was in her car waiting for me. I got up, walked over to her car, and got in.

She looked at me for a minute without pulling out. "Elizabeth, did you get out early," she asked. "The bell hasn't even rung yet."

I looked up and around. There were no students walking around yet. I thought quickly, trying to come up with an excuse for why I was waiting before school got out. I could say I was sick, but then she would ask if I had gone to the nurse. I couldn't think of anything better, so I opened my mouth to tell her I wasn't feeling well, but as soon as I did, I burst into tears.

My mom didn't ask me anything or say anything. She just reached over, rubbed my shoulder, and then drove home. When we got home, she drew me a hot bath and told me to soak for a bit while she got dinner ready. The rest of the night seemed dim in my mind. I think we had soup for dinner, but I really don't remember. All I remember is burying my head in my pillow after dinner and crying myself to sleep.

Chapter 10
Do The Math

The next morning, I forced myself to get up and get ready for school. Any thoughts that my mom would relent on my grounding because of pity for me went out the window when I came downstairs and saw that she was ready to go, dressed in a black skirt, red top, and black high heels. Her purse was on the table, so I knew she was ready, and I was running behind, but she didn't say anything about my being late. She drove a little faster and we still got to school on time. I made it through my morning classes, but I don't remember much about them. We had a surprise quiz in calculus class, but I don't even remember what was on the test.

At lunchtime, I walked slowly to meet Rebecca because I knew what she would ask. She was sitting on the steps of the library, eating a bag of chips, waiting for me.

"Hey, Elizabeth. Where's your lunch? How was your weekend? Did you find out anything about Blake's mom?"

I hesitated, wondering how much I should tell her. I decided to just tell her the bare minimum, but once I started, I told her everything. I told her about finding out Blake's mom had died, about Blake's reaction, about not knowing where Blake and I stood.

Rebecca was great. She didn't interrupt. She just listened. Afterward, she offered me a Kleenex to wipe my eyes which were wet again, and said, "Well, that explains it."

"Explains what?" I asked curiously.

"Every day since your grounding, Blake has found me in the mornings at the student store while I waited for it to open, and he's asked how you were doing. Except today. Today, he was a no-show."

I thought about what this might mean. Were Blake and I over, or did Blake just need time to process the news about his mom? His reaction was so over-the-top and out of character that I really didn't know what he could be thinking at this point. I had tried to rescue him from his pain and doubt, but instead, I had brought more pain to him. The worst part, I thought to myself, was that there was nothing I could do to make it better. This was a problem I couldn't solve. No amount of studying or thinking could help me find a solution.

The bell rang, signaling the end of lunch, so we said goodbye and headed off to our classes. Rebecca hadn't even asked about calculus, and I had forgotten to tell her about the surprise quiz. Of course, my next class was science with Ms. Hart, and we had a surprise quiz in her class, too, which Rebecca hadn't mentioned, so I figured we were even.

The whole rest of the week sort of melted together. I somehow made it to all my classes, did my homework without really thinking about it, and every day at lunch, I asked Rebecca if she had heard from Blake. Every day, she reported that she was sorry but that she hadn't seen nor heard from him. I thought about risking a call or text to him, but I thought maybe it was better to give him time to come to grips with his mom's death.

On Friday morning, I got ready for school extra early. Since my grounding was officially over today, I thought I would drive myself to school early and try to find Blake to talk things through. I knew that night, that Rebecca would be expecting me to go with her to look at this Blood Moon thing, so I wanted to find out what was going on with Blake and me as soon as possible.

Of course, he could have reached out to me but didn't. I know in the beginning he had kept his distance out of respect for my parents and their rules, but I didn't think that was the reason for his distance now. For some reason, he was still upset with me. I knew telling him that his mom had passed away would bring unspeakable grief to him, but he had to understand that I did it because I cared for him. So much pain had crossed his face that I wanted to take it back, but over and over, I came to the same conclusion. I had done the right thing by telling Blake about his mom. Even if I lose him over this, I told myself.

Deep down, if I admitted it, I more than cared for him. If I was being honest, I had fallen deeply for him. That's part of why I felt like I had to tell him. I couldn't have something between us that I knew but was keeping from him. If he cared for me the way I cared for him, then I knew he would eventually see it the same way.

I went downstairs early, figuring I would grab breakfast at the student store before talking to Blake. My mom was sitting at the table drinking coffee and eating a raspberry danish while looking at a crossword puzzle book. Her pencil was poised above the page as if she were ready to write a word but wanted to make sure it was the right word first. I knew from past experience that she was stressed out about something. She only bought Danishes when she was stressed out. She used to buy pastries every Monday on her way to work, and when she quit work, she continued the tradition at home but switched to raspberry danishes since we couldn't eat a whole box of assorted pastries. When she and my dad tried having another baby a few years previously, she had been eating them every day, thinking the extra fat would help her in some way--and it did--until she miscarried and lost the baby. That was when the tradition stopped. Now she only bought them when she was really stressed out and worried about something.

"Mom, is everything okay?" I asked.

She looked up from her crossword and forced a smile that I could tell was not genuine. "Sure, hon. I'm just finishing up this crossword before we go. Don't worry, I'll be ready in time."

I looked at her, confused. She kept looking down at her crossword which I could tell now was blank. She was just using it for a cover to have something in her hands. "I'm not sure what you mean," I began. "I'm going to drive myself today. My grounding is over."

She continued to look down for a minute. I saw her take a deep breath and let it out slowly before she said anything.

"Honey, your grounding isn't over until tomorrow."

I stood there for a minute, trying to comprehend what she had said. "Wait, that doesn't make sense," I said, my voice already rising. You said two weeks. It's been two weeks."

"It began on Saturday," she replied calmly. "I think if you do the math, you'll see that a week is seven days, and two weeks would end after 14 days, not 13."

"But Rebecca is expecting me to go to this thing tonight," I spat out, clearly angry now. "I also need to talk to Blake to clear up a misunderstanding we had."

My mom's eyes narrowed when she heard Blake's name as if she were waiting for it. "How did you have a misunderstanding if you haven't spoken to him while you've been grounded?" she demanded.

My heart raced. I was filled with a mixture of dread and anger. My mom had figured it out and found a crack in which to trap me, but I also felt anger that I wouldn't be seeing him tonight, and I felt this extra punishment was unjust.

"Mom, you don't understand," I began. "It's about Blake's mom. She died, and we had a fight about it."

"So you were talking to him even though you were prohibited from seeing him or talking to him? What other rules have you broken while you were grounded?" she asked. "I'm going to talk to your father to see if we need to extend your grounding since you lied to us and broke the rules."

I knew nothing I said would help the matter, so I stopped talking and stood there. My mom sat for a minute, staring at me before saying, "Be ready to leave at 7:30."

I stormed upstairs to wait. I was so angry that I knew I had to calm down before I said something that would get me into real trouble.

CHAPTER 11
BLOOD MOON

We arrived at school just as the bell rang to go to the first period. I got out of the car and ran to class without saying a word to my mom. The day seemed to speed by while at the same time trudging along at a snail's pace. Somehow, it was going faster and slower at the same time. I kept thinking about Blake expecting to see me tonight at the game and being disappointed when he saw I wasn't in the stands. At least, I hoped he would be disappointed. I wondered if it was wrong for me to hope he would be disappointed when he didn't see me. I decided it didn't matter. Nothing I did right now could change the situation. I would just have to hope he would be understanding for one more day and that we could talk things out on Saturday--that was hoping I didn't have more days added to my punishment.

By lunch, I had gotten three text messages from Rebecca, but I had ignored them, thinking it would be better to talk to her during lunchtime. I was afraid if I started explaining things via text messages, we would be going back and forth for a long time, and I didn't know if I could handle the slow, drawn-out conversation about everything that had happened.

The Fourth period came at last, and I met Rebecca outside of the library. Somehow we both knew to come here instead of the student store. I told her everything that had happened, including the fight with Blake after my telling him that his mom had died.

The first thing she said was, "Elizabeth, who is going to go with me to see the Blood Moon tonight?" after I told her I couldn't and that I was sorry, she seemed to take it okay. After a couple of minutes, she came back with, "That doesn't make any sense. Why would Blake act like that?"

"I don't know," I replied. I've been trying to figure it out. It just doesn't make sense to me."

"How did she die?" Rebecca asked.

I hadn't thought about that. At the time, I didn't think it mattered. "I really don't know," I answered. "The paper didn't say."

"Do you think he already knew?" she asked.

This hadn't even occurred to me. When I had told Blake, he didn't really seem surprised by the news, just upset at me knowing and bringing it up. "That's a possibility, but it still doesn't add up," I said.

The rest of the lunch period, I tried to puzzle it out now that I had a different possibility. As soon as we had finished talking about Blake, she had immediately switched to talking about the Blood Moon and how cool it was going to be and how sorry she was that I was going to miss seeing it with her. Thankfully, I had never told her that I had planned on going out with Blake after the game and would not be watching the Blood Moon with Rebecca. She said that she would miss me but that she thought she would be okay because the Blood Moon would probably keep the vampires away.

It was nice to see her so excited and happy.

After school, I knew my mom would be waiting to pick me up promptly, so I hurried to the curb by the quad where I knew she would be. I had calmed down a lot since that morning, but when I got back into the car I couldn't keep myself from becoming angry again. When I had thought about it, I realized that she was right and that was part of what upset me, as irrational as that seemed. If Blake had helped me relax, open up, and see that there was more to life than studying, my mom had brought out an absurd, illogical, and foolish side of myself that I didn't like. I decided there was nothing else I could do other than accept it and try to change my behavior.

When we got home, I decided I needed to start by apologizing to my mom. I told her that I was sorry that I had felt and behaved very childish lately and that I would do my best to try to change and act more responsibly.

She looked at me and I could tell she was trying to decide if I was being genuine or if I was just saying what she wanted to hear. After a minute, she thanked me, gave me a hug, and said she loved me and only wanted what was best for me. I didn't feel like arguing with her about what was best for me, so I just hugged her back and went upstairs to start my homework. I wanted to have everything done so I could get up early and spend the whole day with Blake if he still wanted to spend time with me. I tried to push doubts out of my head as I opened my calculus book.

As I worked, my mind kept wandering, and I thought about Blake and how disappointed he would be at not seeing me in the stands. I thought about texting him, but I didn't want to give my mom any additional excuses to extend my grounding just in case she asked for my phone.

At 4:30 my dad knocked on my door and said he came home early to take my mom out to dinner. He asked if I was okay and if I wanted to go with them, but I politely declined and said they deserved a night out together.

I went downstairs and made myself a peanut butter and apricot/pineapple jam sandwich and grabbed a box of Cheez-Its out of the pantry. After I finished eating, I tackled English, science, and history/government. I didn't really have homework per se, but I always studied the chapters we covered in class and read ahead to familiarize myself with the upcoming material.

I finished up around 9:45. My parents still weren't back and I was trying to think of something else to do to take my mind off Blake. I thought about what Rebecca had said. How had his mom died? I opened my laptop and pulled up the obituary. It didn't mention anything about how she died. I sat for a minute, reading it over a couple of times to make sure I hadn't missed anything. I remembered there was also a news story in SONDs that mentioned her. I quickly brought up the story and began skimming through it.

My eyes stopped on one sentence near the beginning:

Constance Ray Patterson died Friday night after taking her own life…found by her son, Blake Patterson…

I stared at the screen in disbelief. Grief sat on my chest like a crushing weight. I didn't know what to think. I couldn't believe what I had just read. It all made sense, Blake's reaction to my bringing it up, his hurt and anger. He had known all along. Why had he said she had walked out on them? I wondered. I thought back and, after a minute, recalled what he had actually said. She had left them.

I couldn't process it. I hurt so much for Blake. I could picture him as a freshman coming home after a game and finding her. He had no friends to talk to. His dad didn't seem to care from what Blake had said. This was the most painful part of Blake's life and I had made him relive it.

My phone chirped and I saw it was a text from Rebecca. I ignored it. She could tell me about the Blood Moon later, I thought.

I thought over and over about what I could do to make it better, but I couldn't think of anything. There was nothing I could do. What can anyone do to make the pain that must be that deep go away? The pain will always be there. It will always be a part of Blake. How he had even managed to keep going was a mystery. He had kept going to high school, had kept his grades up enough to stay eligible for football, and had kept going without being able to talk about or share this with anyone. He had lost the most important person in his life. She had left him, abandoned him. I could only just begin to imagine how he felt.

My phone chirped again, and I picked it up, annoyed. I opened it and saw two texts from Rebecca a few minutes apart:

need help field
E where RU

I closed my laptop and ran downstairs, grabbing my keys as I flew through the door. For a brief moment, I thought about leaving a note for my mom and dad so they would know where I was when they got back and saw my car wasn't in the driveway, but I knew there wasn't time. I had to get to Rebecca as quickly as I could. I could tell from her short texts that this wasn't some bogus vampire scare. Rebecca was terrified and in real trouble. I only hoped I could get to her in time.

Once I started driving, I realized right away what my mistake was. Where was I driving? I had no idea where Rebecca was. She had mentioned this Blood Moon thing several times but had never said exactly where she was going to view it. I racked my brain, trying to figure out where she could be. She could have gone to the observatory, but she had said she would be alone if I didn't go with her. Her text had said *field*.

I thought for a few minutes as I drove in a random direction. I had to figure this out, I thought. Rebecca wouldn't go out into the countryside because she didn't like the outdoors and because she would be afraid to be too alone. She would go somewhere she knew. She would go somewhere there weren't any people but somewhere not too far away from people because she would reason that having people close by--even if they weren't in the same direct areas--would keep away the vampires and other fictitious monsters. Sometimes Rebecca could be so smart and insightful, but other times she could be so stupid, I thought. Of course, I had always played along with her because I had never known whether or not she truly believed it or if she was just putting on a game, a type of show to see if she could get others to believe.

She would go somewhere very familiar, I thought. She was always timid and a little fearful of her own shadow when she was alone, so she would definitely pick a familiar place. It suddenly hit me where she would feel comfortable--a place she would feel confident enough to go by herself, but a place somewhat desolate this time of night. She would be at school.

I sped up as I turned north to drive toward school and the football field. Our house was 15-20 minutes away from school, but I had, by chance, driven mostly north, so it was only 10 minutes more before I screeched to a halt on the curb next to the Quad, close to where my mom had been dropping me off.

I got out of the car and looked around. It was 10:20, but it was surprisingly bright, even with most of the lights turned off. There was one dim yellow sodium light in the parking lot, but most of the other lights around the school had been shut off since the game had ended long beforehand. I saw Rebecca's H3 still in the parking lot. I thought about walking over to see if she was in her car, but her text had said field, so I started walking toward the football field. As I passed the science and history buildings, I kept walking right in the middle, afraid if I went too close to one building or the other that something or someone would jump out at me. I scolded myself for being silly, trying to convince myself that everything was safe. Everything was normal.

I came to the entrance to the football field. I had come this way because I thought the gate on the north side might be locked, and I didn't want to have to circle back, even though it would have been much faster to park right by the tunnel entrance if it had been open. I had never been here so late, so I didn't know what to expect, and I didn't want to waste time going to the tunnel, which might or might not have been accessible.

I stepped off the curb and started walking over the track that surrounded the field. I could only see part of the field through the visitor's bleachers. I continued walking slowly as I stepped onto the grass and passed through the gap in the bleachers. I didn't see Rebecca anywhere. I called out to her in a half whisper-half yell. My heart was pounding in my chest and my mouth was so dry I couldn't even swallow.

I looked over to the home side of the field and saw the tunnel cutting under the concrete stadium bleachers. Everything looked deserted. I kept walking until I stopped at the middle of the 40-yard line near the center of the field. I turned around and looked at each goalpost and then turned back to look back at the visitor's bleachers. Even with the bright moon, the stadium was heavy with shadows. Near the far end of the field, I thought I saw a dark shape next to the trash cans. I started walking towards the shape, and soon, I was running. The closer I got, the more I could tell the dark shape was a person lying on the ground.

I stopped 10-15 feet away. It was Rebecca. I half ran--half dropped down next to her, and started crying when I saw the condition she was in. She lay unconscious, her left eye purple and swollen shut. Both cheeks were bruised, and her left cheek was split open and bleeding. Her bottom lip had broken open, and thick blood oozed out. Her hair was caked in blood, and her face was lying in enough blood to send me into a panic.

I quickly dialed 911 on my phone and shook Rebecca, trying to revive her as I screamed into the phone for help. The operator said something to me, but I dropped the phone and tried again to revive Rebecca. Her school shirt was torn half off, exposing her chest, her pants were down past her knees, and her underwear was pulled down and half torn off. Even her legs were bruised and red as if someone had taken the time to punch or kick them.

As I waited for paramedics to come, I looked around for something to cover her with. Her Levi's jacket was a few yards away in the grass. I didn't want to leave her, but I quickly ran over, grabbed her jacket, and draped it over her as best I could. I tried again to revive her, but she was out cold. I didn't know if it was better for her to be awake so that I knew she was okay or if it was better that she was passed out and not feeling any pain.

My phone buzzed, and I pulled it out. It was a text from my mom that just said:

Where are you?

I ignored the text. I decided to roll Rebecca onto her back so her face wouldn't be lying in blood. I rolled her over so that her head was in my lap. I could feel blood soaking through my jeans, but I ignored it. Rebecca's hair had stuck to her face because of the blood, and I brushed it off while trying to see where the blood was coming from. I could see a large gash behind her left temple running back to above her ear. I put my hand on the open wound to try to stop the bleeding, but it kept flowing.

I didn't know what else to do, so with my free hand, I picked up my phone and texted Blake:

Rebecca hurt. football field. need help.

After this, I just held Rebecca's head on my lap and waited for the help that seemed like it would never come.

CHAPTER 12
HEARTACHE

The first to arrive was a fire truck. I saw them pause at the big double gates at the end of the field. Someone got out, cut the lock, and they drove right up to where we were. They got out and immediately started asking questions. A police car and ambulance came a couple of minutes later while they were still asking questions and assessing the situation. One firefighter with latex gloves handed me a bandage type of cloth and told me to put pressure on Rebecca's head with the compress. The police came up and started asking the same questions, and I started over while one paramedic got out of the ambulance and started putting a neck brace on Rebecca, and the other wheeled a gurney over to her.

The police officer kept asking me what happened while I watched the paramedics check over Rebecca. One was shining a flashlight in her eyes while thumbing her eyelids open. The other was setting up a portable IV.

Finally, I looked up as the police officer put a hand on my shoulder and said, "Miss, I need you to focus on me and tell me what happened."

I mumbled something about not really knowing what happened, but I still couldn't focus. I wasn't sure what had happened. A female officer came over and wrapped a silver blanket around me. I didn't feel cold--I didn't feel anything--but I was shivering.

It was clear that Rebecca had been beaten and raped. At first, I couldn't think of anyone who would have hurt Rebecca, but then my mind flashed to Joey and Kenny MacGruber. I couldn't think of anyone else who could have done it. I looked over at Rebecca, who was still unconscious, as they lifted the gurney up and wheeled her to the back of the ambulance.

"Where are they taking her?" I asked. "Is she going to be okay?"

"They're taking her to St. Mary's Trauma Center," replied the female officer. "Can you tell us her name? Can you tell us your name? Maybe tell us what you two were doing out here and who attacked you?

I swallowed, and my throat felt dry and scratchy as I told them who I was, Rebecca's name, and what she had been doing here. I told them about the text I had gotten and what little else I knew, which was nothing. I was about to tell them about Joey and Kenny MacGruber when there was a commotion from over by the firetruck.

A couple of the firemen were trying to stop someone from getting through. I looked over and saw that it was Blake. He finally just pushed his way through and walked briskly toward me. One of the police made as if he was going to try to stop Blake, but decided to let him through--probably not wanting to confront him. Blake had that distant look of anger in his eyes as he looked over at Rebecca being loaded into the back of the ambulance.

He knelt down beside me, put his arms around me, and said, "Are you okay?"

I tried to answer, but suddenly, I was sobbing, so I just nodded into his chest as he held me against him. The police officers must have decided they had everything they needed for now because they walked a few feet away and started talking and writing notes on their little notepads.

Blake just held me as I cried. It felt like hours but was probably just a few minutes. Eventually, I pulled back a little and dabbed my wet eyes and cheeks with a handkerchief Blake handed me.

"I'm so sorry," I began.

He looked at me, confused at first. "You don't have anything to be sorry about," he said. "We'll talk about that later. Right now, I want to get you home."

"I want to go to the hospital with Rebecca," I replied.

"We can do that," he answered. "Let's go." He helped me up and held onto me as we walked.

I was more shaky than I thought I would be, so I was glad to have Blake to steady me. As we walked away the police called out that they needed more information. Blake called back and said that they had our names and could talk to us tomorrow but that he was taking me to the hospital and then home.

He drove behind the ambulance, and when we got to the trauma center, they wheeled Rebecca in while the nurse asked me more questions. Blake asked me for the number of Rebecca's parents and then stepped aside to call them, tell them what had happened and to come to the hospital. I drew strength from how calm and collected he was. I could still tell he was angry, and he had a distant rage behind his eyes, but I could tell he was holding it in check as he dealt with the current situation. I was sure he thought the same thing I did--it was Joey and Kenny MacGruber who had done this. I wanted to get back at them and make them pay for what they did, but at the same time, I didn't want Blake to get hurt or get into trouble. I thought about saying something, but I decided right now, I just had to think about Rebecca and not worry about anything else.

Blake held my hand as we sat in the waiting area in silence. My phone buzzed a couple of times, and I looked to see texts from my mom saying:

The longer you wait, the more trouble you will be in

Answer me

I ignored the texts for now, knowing that I would have to explain everything eventually.

After about 15 minutes, I saw Rebecca's dad walking down the hallway. He spotted me, and as he walked over to me I could tell from his expression that he was surprised and confused to see me there.

"Elizabeth, is everything okay?" he asked, looking down at me. I looked over at Blake. Blake stood up, introduced himself as one of Rebecca's friends, and began to tell Rebecca's dad that Rebecca had been attacked. About the time he finished, Rebecca's mom showed up. She came right over to us in a panic.

"I got a call that Rebecca was here," she said to her husband, alarm clear in her voice. "Was there an accident? Is she okay?" she demanded.

Rebecca's dad looked up, thanked us, and led his wife away, telling her what had happened. We could hear Rebecca's mom cry out a sob as they turned and walked around the corner of the hallway.

After another half hour, Rebecca's dad came back alone. We stood up as he approached us and waited for him to speak.

"Thank you both for helping Rebecca. The doctors say she sustained a pretty serious concussion, and she suffered some pretty serious trauma. She's undergoing some tests to make sure there's no internal damage to her kidneys or organs, but it looks like she'll be okay physically. Do you two know who did this or what happened? Have you spoken to the police?

Blake and I looked at each other, wondering how much to say. I could tell Blake thought the same thing I did, that Joey and his brother Kenny had done this, but we had no proof, no way of telling for sure. I told Rebecca's dad just that I had received a text from Rebecca asking for help and that I had found her on the field. I left out some details that he would be better off not knowing unless Rebecca decided to tell him later. While I spoke, I kept thinking about whether or not to tell him about Joey and Kenny, but in the end, I decided it would serve no purpose. I could talk to the police the next day after I talked with Blake and heard what he thought about it.

Rebecca's dad thanked us and told us we could go home and that he would call me tomorrow with an update as to how Rebecca was doing. Blake and I walked toward the door and Blake took off his letterman's jacket and draped it around my shoulders as we walked through the sliding doors into the cold night air.

My car was still at the school so Blake would have to drive me home in his truck, which I was glad of even though it meant a possible confrontation with my parents. I wanted to stay close to Blake for as long as possible. I knew that when I got home, there was a good possibility that I would be grounded for another two weeks, possibly longer. We drove in silence for a few minutes more, and soon, the silence started to become uncomfortable.

I wanted to just ride with Blake, hold his hand, and not risk it coming to an end, but soon, the quiet became unbearable, and I knew I had to say something. "Blake, first let me say I'm sorry," I began.

"You don't have anything to apologize for. I'm the one who needs to apologize. I shouldn't have reacted that way. I shouldn't have shut you out. I've just been so alone for so long. It's difficult for me to remember that I have someone else in my life now," he said.

This caught me off guard. I was a part of Blake's life. I felt a warmth in my chest that spread throughout my whole body. I was a part of Blake's life. Blake gripped my hand tighter, and I looked over at him. His eyes looked watery, and his expression looked like he was in pain. He continued to grip my hand tightly.

"When my mom first left us…when she killed herself, I was the one who found her. Did you know that? I came home from a game and found her. She never missed one of my games, and I was worried because it was the first time she ever missed, so I hurried home, and I found her. She gave me the football the night of the game and then I came home later and found her." A tear slowly edged over the corner of his eye and slid down his cheek. "I didn't know what to do, so I waited for my dad to come home. When he came home, he was drunk as usual and just told me to take care of it. I was 15. I didn't know what to do, so I called the police, and they came and took away the body and made a report, I guess, and that was all. We didn't have a funeral…nothing. It was as if it never happened. It was as if she never existed. She was the only person who ever believed in me, and suddenly, she was gone, and I had nobody."

My heart felt like it was being crushed in a vice. I was still reeling from earlier, and this was squeezing my emotions so hard that it felt like every breath stung. I wanted to say something, but I couldn't think of anything, so I just squeezed his hand back.

"I felt so alone for so long. I almost joined her. Did you know that? I felt so alone that I considered suicide myself, but then I'd be gone, and nobody would remember me, just like nobody remembers my mom…except me. And then I saw you one morning…and I remembered you from before when we were younger. I remembered your kindness. So many people wanted something from me, but you just wanted to be kind. I can't believe I even thought about IT now. Everything is different now. No more walls. No more keeping people out…at a safe distance. You rescued me, Beth. Even if you move away and I never see you again, I'll never be the same. You rescued me."

I was crying now. I ached to say something, but my voice caught in my throat and came out as a strangled sob. Blake turned and looked at me and then smiled, which made me smile back. I knew everything was going to be alright between us, no matter what. Blake had changed me, too. Blake had rescued me from books and tests and things that I thought I loved, but I now knew were ambitions I used to control things and hide behind. If Blake hid behind his wounds and built walls to keep people out, I had done the same with books and numbers and school.

I could think of nothing else to say, so I said what was deep in my heart, "I love you, Blake."

His crooked smile grew even bigger. "I hope so, Beth, because I love you too."

I scooted over in the bench seat of the truck and leaned into him. He put his arm around me, and I breathed in deeply the smell I had come to associate as his--of clean soap and something floral mixed with the smell of cedar wood. I closed my eyes and felt safer and more comfortable than I think I ever had.

It was past midnight when Blake pulled up to our house. I sat up surprised and asked, "Wait, how did you know where I live?"

"Don't think I'm a stalker or anything, but when you were grounded, I asked Rebecca where you live, and I drove by here once or twice to see if I could catch a glimpse of you." His smile took on a mischievous look.

The front door of our house opened, my mom came out onto the porch, and I knew immediately by her expression that I was in serious trouble.

"Uh oh," I murmured as I sat up and reached for the door handle.

To my surprise Blake got out before I could and came around and opened my door. He grabbed my hand and walked me to where my mom was standing. She stood there, not saying anything.

My mom looked at me strangely and asked, "Elizabeth, are you alright?"

Suddenly, I couldn't talk. I wanted to tell her everything--what happened to Rebecca, how Blake had opened up to me, how scared I was, and how sorry I was for how I had treated her--but I just froze, unable to talk.

"She's okay," Blake finally said. "The blood's not hers."

I looked at Blake questioningly. I didn't know what he was talking about until he nodded toward my arms. Both hands had dried blood on them, and my arms had patches of dried blood smeared from my wrists up past my elbows. Suddenly, it hit me again, and the whole night came crashing down on me. I felt shaky and lightheaded. Blake must have sensed something because he put his arm around me and kind of held me up just in case.

My mom looked at me with a worried look but said nothing for a minute. Finally, she looked at Blake and said, "Thank you for bringing her home safely."

Blake didn't seem surprised at all. He just said good night to my mom and told me to rest and call him the next day if possible. As he let go of me and turned to go, I felt like a piece of me was leaving with him. I watched as he got back in his truck and drove away.

Then, I turned around and prepared to face my mom. I expected the yelling to start, or at the very least, I expected her to tell me how disappointed she was in me, but she just stepped forward, wrapped her arms around me, and hugged me. That was all it took for me to break down and start sobbing again.

We walked slowly into the house and sat down at the kitchen table. She poured two cups of hot water from the kettle on the stove into two mugs and put an orange blossom tea bag in each. I took a big gulp of tea even though it burned my mouth. It seemed to calm me instantly, and I began telling my mom everything that had happened that night.

151

CHAPTER 13
VISITING HOURS

The next morning, I woke up after 8, which was uncharacteristically late for me. Even on Saturdays, I was always up and about by six, seven at the latest. My plan was to eat a quick breakfast and then head to the hospital to see if I could find out how Rebecca was doing. As I walked down the stairs, I thought I heard laughter coming from the kitchen. There was something odd about the sound that seemed out of place.

I turned the corner and spotted Blake and my mom sitting at the table together. I froze in surprise as both turned to look at me. I realized I was still in my pajamas, hair not combed, teeth not brushed--a complete mess. I started to back away, but my mom spoke before I could disappear. "Good morning, sleepyhead. Come have some breakfast."

I decided that Blake had already seen me and besides, I really wanted to spend every bit of time with him that I could. Plus, I wanted to find out what was going on. I felt like I was in some mirror universe or in the Twilight Zone. "Good morning, Mom." I turned to Blake and said, "Good morning, Blake. Don't take this the wrong way…I'm glad to see you, but what are you doing here?"

"Your mom invited me," Blake replied with a big smile on his face. "Thanks again, Mrs. Peterson." My mom just smiled at me.

I was still trying to make sense of it when my mom said, "You left your phone down here, and after our conversation last night, I thought I should have him over so we could get to know each other and talk."

I looked to where my mom pointed at the table where my phone lay. "How did you even know my password?" I asked.

"Please," my mom said, "It was the first thing I tried. 31415. The first five digits of PI. I know you too well, Elizabeth." She smiled big when she said this. "You're very predictable, you know."

"And now I know you very well, too," Blake said, looking at a book in front of him on the table. To my horror, I saw that he had been looking through an old photo album of me. I didn't remember what pictures were in it, but I would bet my mom would have brought out the album with the most embarrassing pictures she could find. I felt my cheeks redden and grow warm with embarrassment as I stepped forward, grabbed the photo album, closed it, and took a step back with it.

"I think you've seen all you're going to see of this," I said, trying to sound authoritative. "And I'm not predictable," I said, turning to my mom.

"If you say so, Elizabeth," she replied while Blake shook, trying to hold in laughter.

Finally, Blake just broke out in laughter and smiled bigger, which added to my embarrassment. I let him laugh for a minute, enjoying the sound of him laughing in our kitchen--a sound I never thought I'd hear--but when it had gone on a little too long, I tried to change the subject. "Any news on Rebecca?"

That sobered everyone up immediately. "Sorry, hun," replied my mom, "No news."

"I thought after you ate, we could go to the hospital," Blake said.

I looked at my mom to gauge her mood. She looked calmer than I had seen her for a long time. "That would be great," I said, turning to my mom, "Unless I'm still grounded..."

"Of course not, Elizabeth," she replied. Of course, my mom would pick now, in front of Blake, to sound reasonable and fair.

I decided it didn't matter. Today was a new day, and my priority was to see how Rebecca was doing. I grabbed two strawberry breakfast bars from the pantry and quickly headed up the stairs, calling back, "Give me five minutes."

Twenty minutes later, we were getting into Blake's truck. The plan was to see Rebecca first and then pick up my car on the way home. I sat right next to him on the bench seat of his truck as he drove to the hospital. When he wasn't shifting, he let his hand rest on my thigh, and I leaned into him, taking in the smell I had come to associate with Blake--clean soap, something floral mixed with the smell of cedar wood.

We got to the hospital just after 9, but visiting hours weren't until 10, so we had to wait. They wouldn't tell us anything about her condition because we weren't related, so we just sat in the waiting area. I held Blake's hand between both of mine and sat with my head leaned against his arm. Strange as it seemed, I was filled with a mixture of anxiety over Rebecca but also a peace from being with Blake again. My mind went back and forth between the horrible image of Rebecca lying in the field, bruised and bleeding, and the conversation I had with Blake that ended with us confessing that we loved each other.

It wasn't long before Rebecca's dad came down the hallway and spotted us. He came up to us and spoke in a low voice, "Have you two been here all night?"

"No, we just got here," I replied. "Any word on how Rebecca is doing?"

He sat down next to us and just looked down for a minute. I was filled with dread, and my anxiety rose with every second, but I knew I couldn't rush his answer. Finally, he spoke in a hushed whisper, "She's in an induced coma. The doctor said there's some swelling in her brain, and one of her kidneys is bruised, but he thinks she'll recover physically. Until she wakes up, we won't know much else. You can go in if you want. Her mom is with her now, but I'll talk to the nurse and tell them it's okay for you to go in to see her," he finished.

I didn't know what to say so we just sat there a couple minutes until he got up and went to the nurse's station. The nurse behind the counter looked over at us and nodded while listening to him. After a couple of minutes, he came back and told us we could go in when we were ready.

Blake stood up and grabbed my hand. I knew I needed to see her--I wanted to see her--but I also had a flashback to the image of her lying in the field, and I knew that when I went in to see her, it would create another image in my mind that I would never be able to get rid of. From the moment I saw her, I would always have that image in my head, just like I would always have the image of her lying in the field, hurt and bleeding.

Blake was still standing and holding my hand, waiting for me to stand. After a few seconds that seemed like hours, I stood up, gripped Blake's hand tighter, and started walking to Rebecca's room.

Her mom had a chair pulled over next to her bed and was holding her hand, talking to her when we went in. She turned and looked at me when we came in. I couldn't tell if the look was just grief and pain over what had happened to Rebecca or if her look contained an accusation as if she thought I should have been with her to stop this from happening, but then she stood up, walked over to me, and hugged me. She shook while embracing me, and I could tell she was crying. Like me, Rebecca was an only child, and I could only imagine the fear and grief she must be experiencing.

After a bit, she stepped away and said, "I'll be outside." Now that we were alone with Rebecca I got my first look at her since the night before. The blood was washed and cleaned off her face and out of her hair, but she looked far worse. Part of her hair on the left side of her head from her temple to just above her ear was shaved off, and I could see where they had used some stitches and surgical staples. Where her face was not purple, it was yellow. Her left eye that had been swollen shut had a gauze bandage taped over it and the white of the bandage contrasted sharply with the dark bruising surrounding the eye. She had a cut on her cheek that had a couple of stitches in it, and both her bottom and top lips were swollen and split open with a vertical scab running through them. An IV was taped to the back of her wrist, and she had a tube taped to her one nostril so that it stayed in place just under her nose.

Just seeing her brought out such raw emotion that I stood stunned in shock. I wanted to cry and shout because looking at Rebecca made me so angry that I could barely contain the storm of emotion coursing through me.

Blake stepped up and, grabbed her hand, and said, "Becca, we're so sorry we weren't there for you. Hang in there. You're going to be okay." His eyes held the same rage that I felt. I realized that this might be just as personal for him. Even though he didn't know Rebecca for very long, he had seen abuse like this growing up. I wondered if seeing Rebecca like this brought up memories of his dad beating him and his mom. He had said his dad had been a mean drunk and had physically assaulted him and his mom while he was growing up--many times sending them to the hospital--until his mom was gone, and he was big enough to fight back and put a stop to it. I didn't know how he could have endured it for so long.

I reached out and put my hand on Rebecca's arm just above Blake's. I wanted to say something, but nothing came to mind. There was nothing I could say to make things better, to make this not happen. If Rebecca got better--when she got better, I told myself--she would still never be the same. Things like this affect the rest of a person's life. It crushes them. Some find the strength to grow past it, but many stay defeated their whole life.

"Keep fighting, Rebecca," I said at last. "We're going to get the people who did this." I don't know what made me say it, but I was so angry that I couldn't think of anything else. Blake looked down at me and rubbed the back of my hand with his thumb.

We stayed another 30 minutes, and then Rebecca's parents came back into the room. They thanked us and told us we could stay, but we wanted to give them time alone with their daughter. I don't know if Rebecca could even sense that we were there, but somehow, I believed she could and that she appreciated it.

When we stepped outside the hospital, the sun was already starting to take the chill off the morning. Before we drove to school to pick up my car, Blake drove us by a little diner he knew, and we had breakfast. I had stuffed a couple of breakfast bars in my pocket earlier but had forgotten all about them. I didn't feel hungry until the food came, and then I was famished, having not eaten anything since the peanut butter and apricot/pineapple jam sandwich the night before. I had waffles with strawberries, and as hungry as I was, I couldn't finish them, but Blake scooped them off my plate when he saw that I had finished. He had ordered pancakes, eggs, bacon and ham, hash browns, biscuits and gravy. I watched Blake eat after I had finished, and I guess that made him self-conscious.

"What? I'm hungry," he mumbled with his mouth half full. He picked up a small piece of sausage and threw it at me playfully. I feigned outrage when it got stuck in my hair, but my mock anger was ruined by my laughter. We had been through so much emotionally that it seemed natural to have this time of relief where we could stop worrying about anything for even a few minutes. The stress lately had become such a weight on my shoulders and I wondered how long Blake had felt this same way. From what he had said, it sounded like this was a normal part of his life. I vowed to myself that I would try to bring as much happiness to his life as possible and, after a minute, vowed the same for Rebecca when she recovered.

Blake drove me home and offered to come in and stay the day with me. I longed to spend the rest of the day with him, but I knew I had to spend time catching up on homework, and more importantly, I had to spend time with my mom, whom I felt I had neglected and mistreated lately.

The rest of the weekend I spent divided between homework, time with my mom, and on the phone with Blake. My first impression of him as a quiet kid who didn't talk much turned out to be wrong. Blake could definitely carry on a conversation, and he was much more intelligent than people gave him credit for. He seemed to know trivia and facts about almost everything. I enjoyed talking with him on the phone almost as much as I enjoyed being with him in person, and I had a sense that he felt the same way. Somehow, as different as we were, we fit.

Monday morning, I drove to school and found him waiting for me bright and early in the parking lot right where I usually parked. He smiled when I got out and I wasn't sure if it was because he was glad to see me or if it was because he liked catching me off guard and surprising me.

"Hi, what's up?" I asked.

"Nothing. I just have extra time, and I'm tired of hiding from everyone." I wasn't quite sure what he meant, but that week, he met me every morning and stayed with me until classes started. He also met me during lunch, which was nice because, without Rebecca, I would have been alone. I didn't mind being alone since I could always study in the library, but the first day when I tried to go to the library, he stopped me.

"I don't think so," he said. "If I can't hide, neither can you. I'm not hiding in the weight room, locker room, or boiler room anymore, so you can't hide in the library anymore. We need to stop hiding and live."

So we got lunch and ate right in the middle of the quad. At first, people left us alone--too surprised to approach us, but by the second day, a steady stream of people came by just to talk or congratulate Blake on the season he was having. He was always gracious and every single time, he stopped and introduced me as his girlfriend, which brought rose blossoms of embarrassment to my cheeks every time. It also brought pride, and with each day, my insecurities melted away. I was becoming more confident interacting with Blake's friends every day. By the end of the day, people I barely remembered meeting started saying hi to me in the hallways.

One day, walking down the halls, I saw a short girl in short blue jeans, a crop top, and a streak of deep blue running through her jet-black hair. "Hey, Perla," I said, glad to finally recognize someone.

She turned and smiled big when she saw who it was. "Hey, Beth," using the name Blake had introduced me as. "Where's Blake? I hear you two are inseparable now." She said it without any of the jealousy or judging that I had learned to recognize from some of the girls who pretended to be friendly with me.

"We have different schedules, but yeah, we've been spending more time together."

"I'm happy for you both," she said with a genuine smile. "I haven't seen him at any parties for a couple of weeks. That's not a bad thing, though. At least now I know why."

"Have there been many parties?" I asked. I knew after the game, Blake would usually go to a party to *make an appearance* and make sure people didn't think he was disrespecting them. I also knew he didn't like going, but felt he had to, and I also knew he hadn't NOT gone because of me. I had been grounded, so if he wasn't spending time at parties, it wasn't because he had been with me.

"Girl, there's parties every night if you know where to look," Perla replied.

I didn't know what to say, so I just nodded. After a minute, I asked, "How's Rory?"

She shook her head slightly as if amused and said, "Girl, we're not exclusive like you and Blake." Again, I just nodded like I knew what she meant.

The bell rang, and we said our goodbyes and went to class. When she turned to go, I noticed that she had shaved the lower three inches above her left ear down to stubble. I wondered if that was somehow to show support for Rebecca, but then realized she didn't know Rebecca and was probably just making a fashion statement.

At lunch, I met Blake at our usual spot. I tried to think of a casual way to ask where he had been hanging out when I was at home grounded, but I couldn't think of a way to bring it up while sounding relaxed and unconcerned, so finally, I just told him what Perla had said. It was better being honest anyway.

Blake just said, "I'm through hiding, and I'm also through pretending. I'm not going to pretend to be the person they want." He took a big bite of his sandwich and said through a mouth half full, "You know, Beth. You don't have to pretend anymore, either."

I was taken aback by this. Was I pretending somehow? I thought about it for a while, and after a few minutes, Blake noticed my silence. "What are you so quiet about?" he asked. "Usually, you're the talkative one," he said, then realizing what he said, he immediately apologized. "I didn't mean to make it sound like you talk too much. I love to listen to you. It's just that you aren't usually brooding like this. What's wrong? Did I say something I shouldn't have?"

"Blake, do you think I'm pretending?"

"Beth, you're the smartest person I know. You would still get straight A's without spending all your time in the library. You're letting life pass you by. You don't need to pretend to be the smartest person at school because everyone already knows you *are* the smartest person at school."

I thought for a moment before answering, "What if that's all I am?"

Blake let out a big laugh and smiled his big crooked smile. "Beth, you are so much more than that. There's so much more to you than brains. You just haven't figured it out yet. You're the only one who doesn't see it."

"You sound like my mom," I said.

Blake smiled even bigger. "That's good because she's just as smart as you so if I sound like her, then I must be getting smarter from hanging around you."

We enjoyed the rest of lunch together and went to our classes after making plans to meet immediately after school. Rebecca's dad had called early that morning and asked us to come to the hospital after school. I would skip the library, and Blake would skip practice.

We got to the hospital at four and went to the nurses' station. The nurse on duty told us to wait while she paged Rebecca's dad. He appeared a couple of minutes later and told us he was glad to see us.

After pleasantries, he said, "Rebecca is awake, so I thought it would do her some good to see you. She's still pretty shaken up, and her memory is a little fuzzy--she forgets things--but all indications are that she should fully recover. Just don't bring up that night, please. She doesn't completely remember what happened, and we think it best if she recovers any memories in her own time so she can cope with them gradually.

We agreed, and he led us to her room. When we went in the room, the lights were dim, and the room smelled like rubbing alcohol or antiseptic. Rebecca looked like she was asleep at first, but as we drew closer, she opened her eyes and looked at us. She didn't smile or show any expression, but just stared at us. I noticed the surgical staples on the side of her head had been removed, and some very neat stitches with tiny thread had replaced them. Rebecca's dad probably threw a fit when he saw them and had probably restitched her cut the first chance he got, even though once the hair grew back, it wouldn't show. Much of her face still looked swollen and puffy with purple and yellow bruises. The bandage was off of her left eye, but it looked very bloodshot. Her lips still had scabs on them where they had split open. Just the sight of her condition made me angry, and I had to take a calming breath before speaking.

"Hi, Rebecca," I said, taking a step forward. Blake came up next to me and grabbed my hand. His hand was warm and comforting. I thought about taking Rebecca's hand but was afraid that if I did, Blake might also take her hand, and I didn't know how she would react to that. I waited a minute and she didn't say anything so I spoke up again. "It's me, Elizabeth. How are you doing?"

She swallowed and waited a few seconds before answering, "I know who you are." After a minute more, she said, "I guess I had an accident. My dad said you were there and that you helped me."

Her dad stepped up just behind us, and I remembered his admonition not to say too much about what had happened. "Yeah, it was pretty scary, but you're going to be okay. You'll be back at school before you know it."

"Daddy said I'm not going back," she replied.

I looked back at her dad, confused. He responded, "Her mother and I think it would be best if she did not return there. We're going to hire a private tutor, and she'll be homeschooled while she recovers. After that, we'll see, but it's very doubtful she'll return."

I should have expected this, but it caught me off guard. This was our last year and we had talked about how fun it would be graduating together and going to some of the end-of-the-year activities together. I wondered how much I would be able to see her once she was home. I had grown used to seeing her every day for years, even on most Saturdays.

Blake spoke up, breaking me out of my thoughts. "Hey, Becca. I brought something for you." He stepped forward and placed his football on the bed beside her next to the railing. It was the football that his mom had given him and I knew how much it had meant to him. "Are you still going to come to the games?"

Rebecca looked at him for a moment before replying, "I'm sorry, do I know you?" Blake looked over at me, unsure what to do.

"Rebecca, you remember Blake, don't you?" I said. I felt like my throat was constricting as I struggled to hold back my emotions.

"I think so," was all she said. The air grew thick with our silence. Nobody said anything for a very long minute.

Rebecca's dad cleared his throat and took a step forward. "Well, thank you for coming by. Rebecca needs her rest, so let's leave her for a while and you can come back in a few days to visit again.

"Thank you, Dr. Swartz," we both said to Rebecca's dad. "Goodbye, Rebecca. Get well," I said at the same time that Blake said, "Take care." When we got outside, we just stood there looking at each other, not saying anything. It was miserable seeing Rebecca like that.

She was usually so spirited and full of enthusiasm. Now, she seemed a cheerless shell of her former self. Her dad had said she would recover eventually, but I wasn't sure if she would ever be the same--and this was without her even remembering the attack. I couldn't begin to imagine the pain and anger that would overtake her once she remembered the assault.

Finally, we started walking to the exit, both of us in subdued, dreary moods.

CHAPTER 14
GAVE OFF A VIBE?

The next day was Friday. Blake and I met before school and talked but didn't mention Rebecca. We were both too depressed and scared to voice what we felt, as if saying them aloud would make what we feared come true. We had to keep hoping Rebecca would be okay eventually.

By lunch, our moods had lightened. We didn't have much time to talk while we ate because people kept coming by and wishing Blake good luck on the game that night. Blake wasn't the only one who got attention. Nearly everyone who stopped to say hello to Blake also said hi to me and called me by name. It was a little unsettling, everyone knowing who I was, but me not really knowing any of them.

At one point, I mentioned it to Blake, and he just said, "Everyone has always known who you are. They were just afraid to approach you. You used to give off a vibe."

I was taken aback by this and told him so. "I gave off a vibe? What kind of vibe? What do you mean?"

"Well, to people who didn't know you--which was pretty much everyone--you gave off a vibe that kind of said, 'I'm busy. I don't have time for friends.'" I stared in shock, and he quickly added, "Hey, I'm just being honest. We said we'd always be honest, right?"

I tried to change my expression to one of indifference. "We did, and I don't mind. I'm just surprised. Did people really see me that way?"

"Beth, you're smart, pretty, and have a great sense of humor. Is there another reason you can think of why boys weren't beating down your door asking you out?" he answered.

I blushed deeply. Even though I had come to believe that he felt that way about me, I still couldn't believe it about myself. To me, I was always just a brain, a human computer. I don't think anyone ever told me I was pretty or funny or anything that Blake had said about me. With all the attention I was getting lately, I was starting to believe what my mom had been telling me all my life.

Blake had changed a lot recently, too. He was still a little quiet and shy--hard as that was to believe--but since we had been talking so much, he had grown in confidence, and I could tell he was starting to believe he was more than just a quarterback. From the beginning, I could tell that Blake was very quick-witted and intelligent, but he had always thought of himself as thickheaded. He seemed surprised when he started getting As on all his tests after we spent just a small amount of time studying. He couldn't believe how little time it took to study and bring his grades up from B's and C's to mostly A's.

At one point, he said, "This is all you do to get A's?" he didn't say it to diminish my grades but was just shocked by his own accomplishments. The truth was most people wouldn't have picked up things so quickly. Most people would have needed to see things 3-4 times, but Blake could usually pick things up the first time, even complicated concepts. It was true that I was in much more advanced classes, but I was starting to believe that Blake could have done just as well in my classes if he had enough time and the precursor classes to build upon.

We were just finishing lunch when I spotted a tall, white-haired boy walking this way. Rory stopped a few feet away and nodded at Blake who got up and said he'd be right back. Blake and Rory walked a few feet away and put their heads together. A couple of times, Rory looked over at me, his pale eyes peering at me from under his blond eyelashes. He was wearing a white tank top under a Levi's jacket. They were far enough away to where I couldn't hear what they were saying but close enough to see the freckles on Rory's face, upper arms, and hands. A couple times Rory looked over at me and shook his head. Blake looked over at me once but tried to make it look like he was just looking around. Finally, Blake and Rory fist-bumped up and down and ended knuckles touching. Rory walked off, and Blake came and stood next to where I was sitting and held a hand out to help me up.

"We better get going," he said. "The bell's about to ring."

I looked at the time on my phone. "How do you do that?" I asked.

He just smiled and helped me up.

As we walked to the edge of the Quad, I asked, "So what did you and Rory talk about?" I could tell by his reaction that he had thought I hadn't noticed being the topic of their conversation.

He didn't answer right away but then said, "I asked him for a favor, that's all." I could tell there was more. We had said we would always be honest and I could tell he was being honest, just holding something back. I knew if it was important or if I pressed him, he would tell me, but I trusted him and let it go. After school, he had to get ready for the game, so we agreed to meet after the game, and I promised to wait in the stands until he came and got me.

I decided to skip the library after school because I figured I could catch up on anything on Saturday and because I really was starting to believe there was more to life than studying. I went home, showered, and got dressed, wearing blue jeans, white tennis shoes, and a purple and gold school T-shirt with the Ridgeview Wildcats logo on it that I had purchased from the student store earlier in the week. I thought about wearing my hair up in a ponytail to expose my neck, but decided it made me look younger so I wore it down and loose around my shoulders. I ate a snack and brushed my teeth so that I wouldn't have to eat at the game. I wanted to make sure my breath was fresh, and I also made sure I had some breath mints in my purse just in case I needed them. I didn't know what Blake had planned for after the game, but I still remembered the last time we had an official date after a game and the titillating sensation when he had kissed me full on the lips.

I was just heading out the door when my mom stopped me. "Elizabeth, are you going to the game tonight?" she asked, knowing I was.

"Yeah, Mom," I replied.

"Are you going to be drinking or doing anything else that will get you into trouble?" she asked.

"No. I learned my lesson," I said to placate her.

"That's good," she murmured. "So, what are you doing after the game?"

Here it was, I thought to myself. This is what she really wanted to ask. "I don't know," I replied. "We might go to dinner, or we might just hang out." After a brief moment, I added, "We definitely won't be going to any parties, so don't worry."

"Well, if you need me or if you need a ride, you have my number," she continued. A minute of awkward silence passed, and I wondered if it was okay to leave or if she was working up to ask something else. Sure enough, the uncomfortable and embarrassing question came. "Do we need to have *The Talk* again to remind you to be careful?" she asked.

When I had turned 15, my mom had decided it was time for me to know certain things about where babies come from and how to keep from becoming spontaneously pregnant. I had already had biology in middle school and knew everything she told me, but I humored her at the time. This time, I definitely didn't want to sit through *The Talk* again.

"No, ma'am," I said. "I remember everything you said before.

She paused for a moment as if trying to decide whether to launch into *The Talk* anyway, but after a moment just said, "Well, be careful with whatever you do tonight."

I promised I would and then quickly left before she changed her mind. I got to the game early and walked along the lower section in front of the concrete bleachers to the northwest side of the stadium, where the door to the locker room was, and sat in the spot where Rebecca and I had sat just three weeks before. So much had happened since then. I sat on the cold, hard concrete seat, telling myself I would bring a seat cushion the next time, even if it did make me look like an old fuddy-duddy.

I was one of the first people to arrive, and the stands were nearly empty. It was a little difficult to sit with nothing to do or look at because my thoughts kept going back to Rebecca. I hoped her memory would come back, but at the same time, I worried what would happen when it did. She had been through such a traumatic experience that maybe it was better to not remember. Maybe it was her brain's way of protecting her. She was always so upbeat and cheerful that it had been difficult for me to see her at the hospital. The light had gone out of her eyes. Even without remembering what had happened, she seemed despondent and downcast. She hadn't remembered Blake at all, and she didn't seem to even want to look me in the eye. I knew the next few weeks would be difficult for her, and I vowed to make time to be there for her.

The crowds slowly filtered into the stands, and the pep band came out and sat in the stands to my left. The people in the stands were all talking, laughing, and waiting excitedly for the game to start. I wondered if any of them even knew what had happened to Rebecca. She had come to every game, but nobody probably even noticed she wasn't here tonight.

The teams came out, and I watched as Blake led the team out of the locker room, bursting through a banner made of butcher paper and running onto the center of the field to the cheers and yells of the crowd. The stadium was packed. I saw Blake look around in the stand and wave to me. I waved back and smiled. A few people looked over at me, but I had grown used to attention and wasn't embarrassed at all. The team went to their side of the field in front of our stands, and Blake stayed on the field with the opposing quarterback. I saw Blake looking up above me and to my left. I turned and saw Rory sitting alone in the stands. There was no sign of Perla, just Rory sitting alone amongst the crowd. The referee called the two quarterbacks to him, flipped a coin, and pointed to Blake, who pointed downfield. I wasn't sure what it all meant, but our team had the ball first, and soon, the other team was kicking the ball to us.

As the night went on, Blake had an amazing night. He threw four touchdown passes and ran with the ball for two more touchdowns. Our team was up by a lot and the crowd was cheering wildly. I was caught up in the excitement and was cheering along with everyone else.

At one point, I looked over at the band as they played "Go, Fight, Win," and saw two people standing at the bottom of the stadium. Even from a distance, I recognized Joey MacGruber and his brother Kenny. Joey was smoking a cigarette and staring right at me through his droopy eyes, a sneer on his face. He elbowed Kenny and nodded in my direction and Kenny looked in my direction too. I got goosebumps and felt frightened and angry at the same time. They noticed me staring at them, and Joey half smiled and half smirked. I tried to turn my look into a glare and tried to convey as much disdain and anger in my gaze as I could. I could see Joey say something to Kenny, and Kenny laughed. After a couple of minutes, Kenny elbowed Joey and nodded, and they walked in my direction before turning to walk through the tunnel that led to the bathrooms and parking lot.

I unclenched my hands that I hadn't even noticed were balled up in tight fists. My hands were shaking, and I tried to take a few calming breaths. The game was almost over, and I watched for a few more minutes, trying to take my mind off of Joey and Kenny MacGruber and the image of finding Rebecca on the field. I decided to get a Coke, thinking the sugar would help me stop shaking. I walked down the stairs and to the left to the concession stand. I was starting to get hungry again but just bought a Coke in case Blake wanted to get something to eat after the game. I knew he never ate before a game and that he would be hungry.

As I drank my soda and watched the last few minutes of the game, I wondered what we would be doing after the game. Blake liked to go to the diner he had taken me to a couple of times for breakfast and once for lunch. They had good waffles and it was open 24 hours. I'd be okay with that, but I would also be okay just sitting in the Quad, alone with Blake. I blushed a little just thinking about sitting alone with Blake on the bench in the Quad.

The game ended with our team pulling out a crushing victory. The crowd cheered wildly as the game ended, and people immediately started walking down the concrete steps to stand and wait to funnel out and exit. I stayed in my seat to wait for Blake. After a few minutes, I watched the last few people filter out through the tunnel. The concrete bench I was sitting on was cold, and I scolded myself for not bringing a jacket. The coke I had drank was also something I was beginning to regret. I really needed to use the restroom. I took out a breath mint and chewed on it while waiting for Blake to come out.

The main field lights shut off leaving only the few secondary lights on, casting the field in a dim yellow glow. I knew those lights would stay on until 10, but they gave off such a minuscule amount of light that they created more shadows than anything else. It was just after nine, and I was really starting to wish Blake would hurry up. I had told Blake I would stay until he came out, but I really needed to go to the bathrooms, and I was worried that if I waited too long, they would be locked, so after another couple of minutes, I stood up and made my way down the stadium to the tunnel that led outside the stadium to the bathrooms.

The tunnel was dim as I walked through it. Two of the three lights had burned-out bulbs. When I stepped outside the tunnel onto the walkway, I looked around. It was just as dim out here as in the tunnel and inside the stadium. The parking lot across the street was empty except for my car. I turned right and started walking the short distance to the restrooms. A movement caught my eye ahead and to the right, just around the corner of the building that was attached to the stadium. It was so dark that I wasn't sure if I had seen someone duck around the corner or if it had been my imagination. I stopped for a minute and waited, but I really needed to go to the restroom before I burst, so I started walking again.

I reached the restrooms and was relieved to find they were still unlocked. I quickly went in, sat on the cold seat, and instantly felt much better. The water was ice cold as I washed my hands and the air dryer didn't help warm them as it blew cold air instead of hot. I stepped back out of the bathroom and spotted a tall figure standing a few yards away just to my right, just standing as if waiting for me.

It was too dark to tell who it was because whoever it was was standing in the shadows next to a mulberry tree. I could tell by his height and frame it wasn't Blake. He was much taller and thinner than Blake. I turned and started walking quickly away. I debated for a minute whether I should run across the street to the parking lot where my car was parked or go back through the tunnel into the stadium to where I hoped Blake would soon emerge.

I looked back behind me and saw the person was walking toward me. My throat grew dry, and I needed to swallow.

I quickened my pace and walked toward the tunnel entrance. I thought about grabbing the gate and closing it behind me as I walked into the tunnel, but there was no way I could lock it since the padlock and chain were wrapped around and locked onto the gate itself. I was halfway through the tunnel when the footsteps behind me told me I was being pursued. Whoever it was, was coming after me. I broke into a run and turned around as I went to see how far the person was behind me.

Suddenly I hit a wall of a person that blocked me from the front. I screamed as I tried to back away, but arms wrapped around me and kept me from escaping. I screamed again and fell back onto my butt as the person released me.

I looked up and could just make out the face of Blake looking down at me.

Chapter 15
Conspiring Together

"Beth, what's wrong?" he asked. It took me a moment to calm down enough to comprehend that it was Blake.

"Blake?" I asked. I knew I sounded childish and as I sat on my butt in the dark tunnel I suddenly became very embarrassed.

He reached down and pulled me up. I immediately hugged him, still shaking from adrenaline. I looked back remembering the person behind me. I still couldn't tell who it was, but it instantly became very clear when Blake called out, "It's okay, Rory. We're okay. Thanks."

I watched to see the outline of the person whom I now clearly recognized as Rory nod and turn to walk back through the tunnel.

I hugged Blake tighter, partially from relief and partially because I was still shaking, and I was afraid if I let go, Blake would see just how frightened I had been, and I thought I had been embarrassed enough for one night. Blake just held on without saying anything, which was another thing on my list of the hundred things I loved about Blake. He knew when to not say anything. He was coming out of a shell that he had built to protect himself from what he imagined would happen if he ever spoke his mind. He had grown in confidence since we had been having such long conversations, but he still knew what I needed, which right then was just to be held until I felt safe--maybe for a few days…or weeks.

Finally, I had calmed down enough and let go. I grabbed his hand in mine, not quite ready to let go completely. We walked the rest of the way through the dark tunnel and out into the fresh night air. I took a deep breath when we stepped onto the curb. I hadn't realized how closed-in the tunnel had felt. Of course, I had never been in the tunnel for more than a few seconds before. For a brief moment I started calculating how long I had been in the tunnel, but I stopped myself. That was the type of coping mechanism I had engaged in before so I wouldn't have to face real issues and problems. The real issue here was that I was afraid. Ever since the night I had seen Rebecca on the field, I had been scared. I was scared she wouldn't wake up. Then I was scared she wouldn't remember me. Then, I was scared of how empty my life would be without her when she didn't return to school. I was tired of being scared, but I knew that since that night, every time I was ever alone at night, I would be afraid, and the memory of Rebecca lying helpless and unconscious would haunt me.

"You don't have to be afraid, Beth. I'll never let anything happen to you," Blake said, interrupting my thoughts. Of course, he knew exactly what I had been thinking. I had forgotten how good he was at reading people.

I squeezed his giant hand tightly as we walked. "I'm not scared," I lied. "Well, I was, but I'm not now," I admitted. I just heard someone following me and then I saw a tall figure, but I didn't recognize it as Rory, so I thought it might be Joey or Kenny MacGruber."

I could tell by the rigidness in Blake's arm that he was angry. "I wish it had been them," he said in a low voice that was almost a growl.

I reached over and rubbed his arm until he visibly relaxed a little. "Sorry," he said. Then, after a minute, he said, "So what should we do tonight?" leaving it up to me. Somehow, I could tell that Blake had made plans for us, but that he had changed them because of what had happened.

I thought for a minute and then answered truthfully, "Honestly, I was hoping we could just spend some time alone together, but now I'm really wanting to be around other people." If Blake was disappointed, he gave no indication. He just nodded and let me across the street to the parking lot where my car was parked.

"Okay, if we take your car?" he asked. "My dad is using our truck. He's actually going to an AA meeting."

"Blake, that's great," I replied, glad to hear some good news for a change.

"We'll see," Blake responded. "This isn't the first time he's said he's quitting. He's 'quit for good' several times in the past."

"Still, it's a step in the right direction," I returned. "You gotta focus on the positive."

"I guess," was all he said. I could tell he was deep in thought as we got into my Honda. We decided to go to the diner to get something to eat. I knew Blake was hungry since he never ate before a game, and the snack I had before leaving the house had long since left my bloodstream. I was famished and I hoped eating something would also help settle me down the rest of the way since I still felt slightly unsteady.

Even though it was nearly 10 when we got to the diner, it was crowded and we had to wait for a table. Blake explained that a lot of people came here because it was open 24 hours and served breakfast all day and night. Once we got a table, I ordered waffles and strawberries again. Blake ordered a double burger, fries, and onion rings, bacon and sausage links on the side, a coke, and a chocolate shake. He saw my expression when he was ordering and winked at me before saying to the waitress, "We'll wait to order dessert until after we're finished with dinner." The waitress gave no indication that she was surprised by his order. She just shuffled off toward the kitchen, leaving us alone to wait for our meal.

Blake looked at me as if he were waiting for me to say something, but I couldn't think of what he would be waiting for me to say. After a minute, it came to me.

"So what was that with Rory," I asked. Blake smiled big, and I knew that he had been expecting me to ask about it. "Did you tell him to follow me, or what exactly?"

"Yes," was all he said at first. I think he was seeing if he could just get away with that, but we'd had too many conversations for me to let that pass. I knew now that he wasn't just the strong, silent type. He had a brain, and he sometimes hid behind the mask of being too shy and quiet to say anything. I knew him better, and so I just stared for a minute without saying anything. It didn't take long.

"Okay, so the first night at the party when I said I needed to talk to Rory?" he started to explain. "I just asked him to keep an eye on you for me. Then, after what happened to Becca, I told him to not let you out of his sight unless I was with you. I'm sorry that I didn't tell you, but I just wanted you to be safe. I never thought you might mistake him for Joey or Kenny," he finished.

"That's okay," I said. "Honestly, I should be mad, but I'm actually a little relieved," I admitted.

"But just for future times, you did say you would wait for me, and then you left before I came out."

"I had to go to the bathroom really badly," I said, heated and embarrassed at the same time. I knew he was right, but I also knew that there wasn't much I could have done differently. Blake nodded and I could tell he wasn't at all upset. He had just been trying to see how I would react. He was very good at getting me to react emotionally. It had been a game he played--trying to get me to react with emotions more and to get out of my head all the time. I had come to realize that I had built up walls to keep people out like Blake had done. Letting Blake in had been easy, but I needed to start opening myself up to other people as well.

I had come to realize that the walls I had put up to protect me had really become walls that had kept me in. Blake had rescued me. He had rescued me from the life of books and the endless studying that I had loved so much because I hadn't allowed anything else. He had rescued me from myself.

Our food came, breaking each of us out of our private thoughts. I took a bite of my waffles with a piece of strawberry. Blake smiled his crooked smile as he watched me take a bite. "What?" I said with a full mouth.

"Nothing," he replied. "You're just predictable," he said and smiled again.

I tried to think of something to say, but all I could think of was, *You're pretty predictable yourself, ordering the whole menu,* but that sounded lame, so I just took another bite and watched as Blake started devouring his meal.

We stayed and talked at the table for an hour after we had finished eating until finally, the waitress said, "Are you two going to order anything else, because we have people waiting for the table."

We looked and saw the crowd had grown even more since we had gotten here. We apologized, paid for our food, left a hefty tip, and left. Blake said we could go somewhere else, but that since it was twenty till midnight, I might not want to press my luck on my first night of freedom. I looked at my watch and saw that it was 11:40. I still didn't know how he did it.

"Oh no, I'm going to be late, and my mom will ground me again," I complained, driving faster to drop Blake off.

"Slow down, your mom isn't going to ground you," Blake replied.

I glanced over at him and saw that he was serious. "How do you know that?"

"Well, I talked with her earlier today and told her we might be late. She said that was fine."

"Of course she did," I responded, slightly annoyed.

"As long as we wouldn't be drinking or anything like that," Blake added. He could tell I was a little irritated. I knew I should have been happy. I could stay out later and not get in trouble, but it annoyed me that my mom was suddenly so reasonable after I had painted her as an authoritarian tyrant.

I was still dwelling over this when Blake leaned over and kissed me. It snapped me out of my thoughts instantly. He started to pull away, but I reached up and, grabbed his head and pulled it back. We enjoyed a long kiss this time and finally, Blake pulled back away.

"I wish we could do this for hours, but we probably shouldn't push our luck," he said. "It's five till midnight, and it takes about 20 minutes for you to get home from here. Even though your mom said you could come home later, I don't think we should risk you coming home too late."

What he said sounded so reasonable, and I found myself nodding in agreement even though I just wanted to lean over and kiss him again. I inhaled deeply so I could remember the smell of clean soap and cedar wood and some kind of floral smell that must have been his shampoo or conditioner.

Finally, he got out, said goodnight through the open window, and walked off. I drove home, still feeling the caress of his lips on mine.

When I got home, my mom was waiting for me at the kitchen table. She had two mugs already full of hot cocoa and I wondered how she had known when I would be coming in. I sat and took a drink of the hot cocoa. It slightly burned my tongue, but I took a deep drink anyway, enjoying the warmth as it went down. My mom just looked at me while I drank. She was being uncharacteristically quiet.

After a couple of minutes, she finally broke the silence, "Good morning, Elizabeth. Did you have a good night?"

I choked on a gulp of coca and coughed a little before answering, "Yes, sorry I'm late."

"That's okay, sweetie. Blake told me you'd be a little late. He texted me a little while ago and let me know you were on your way."

So that was how she knew when I'd be home, I thought. I smiled as I thought of Blake and my mom conspiring together. I couldn't be upset with them. They were just showing they cared about me. I waited for my mom to ask me more questions. I figured I was in for a grilling.

Instead, my mom just stood up, and took her mug to the sink to rinse it out. She came back and kissed the top of my head and said, "Well, I'm glad you had a good time, and I'm glad you're home safe. See you tomorrow…well, later today, I guess." With that, she left me alone in the kitchen, wishing I could call Blake and ask him how he had managed such a change in my mom.

I went up to bed and closed my eyes, remembering the feel of Blake's lips on mine, and I drifted off to sleep, dreaming I was still in my car parked in front of Blake's apartment, embracing him, stirred deeply by his touch.

CHAPTER 16
STRAWBERRIES AND WAFFLES

The next morning, I woke up early but lay in bed for a while, still thinking about the night before. Even though the evening had started off on a bad note, by the end of the night, it had turned out perfect. I would endure being scared like that again if it meant I could spend another night like that with Blake. It didn't matter if we spent time together eating in diners, talking in the Quad, or kissing in the car. I had come to appreciate every moment with Blake. While I might have preferred more *alone* time with Blake, even the time in the diner watching Blake eat, laughing with him, and seeing him happy and relaxed was elation.

After a few more minutes, I got up and headed downstairs for breakfast. I walked into the kitchen and was surprised again to see Blake sitting at the breakfast table with my mom. He looked up at me and smiled broadly.

"Good morning, Beth," he said with a mouth full of waffles. "Your mom invited me to breakfast again." He smiled even broader.

I decided there was no reason to go back upstairs to brush my hair and change, so I just came in and sat next to him at the table. Besides, I decided it was nice seeing him first thing in the morning.

My mom came over and set a plate of waffles in front of me. "Good morning, *Beth*," she said with a smirk on her face. As long as I'd been alive, she had never called me that. I could tell she was enjoying seeing me flabbergasted and unprepared. I looked at Blake, poured some syrup on my waffles, and decided it didn't bother me a bit.

"Do we have any strawberries to go with the waffles?" I asked.

"Strawberries?" asked my mom, "on waffles?"

"Nevermind," I said and took a big bite as I watched Blake do the same.

My dad came into the kitchen just then, dressed for work even though it was Saturday. He leaned over and kissed me on the top of the head and said, "Good morning, everyone. Good morning, Blake."

Blake replied, "Good morning, sir. Thanks for having me over."

"Of course," my dad replied. "Call me David." He turned to my mom and apologized, "Sorry, Ann, no waffles for me. I have to head to the office to put out a couple of fires. I'll be back before lunch, I hope."

My mom protested a little like she always did, but soon, he headed out. I knew he would be back after lunch, sometime just before dinner. My mom brought two mugs of tea over and sat one in front of Blake and one in front of me before grabbing one more for herself and sitting down across from us. I looked over at her, trying to convey by my stare my desire for her to go upstairs and leave Blake and me alone so we could have some time together, but she either couldn't read my expression or, more than likely, she decided to ignore it.

We spent the morning eating, talking, and laughing. After breakfast, I excused myself, went upstairs to change and freshen up, and then came back downstairs. Blake and my mom were still sitting at the table talking. The conversation paused when I came into the room and I became self-conscious, but soon the conversation started up again. My mom had cleared the breakfast dishes and we sat and talked all morning. Even with my mom there, it was relaxing and satisfying. I realized that when I was with

Blake, I felt comfortable. It didn't matter who else was around--even my mom. I was content.

I usually spent all day Saturday studying, but I blew it off, thinking I would just catch up on Sunday, but Sunday morning I came down to find Blake at the table again, smiling his crooked smile even wider. This time, my dad stayed and we spent the whole day talking and just enjoying each other's company.

The next week was much like the previous one. Blake met me before school and during lunches. I studied after school extra hard to try to catch up with what I imagined I had missed during the weekend, but I found that I got the same grades on my assignments and tests that I always managed to. Maybe Blake was right, and I didn't really need to study as much as I thought I did. Maybe I could spend even more time with Blake, I imagined. My cheeks grew hot thinking about what we could do with the extra time together.

On Thursday morning, I had received another call from Rebecca's dad asking if we wanted to come by and visit Rebecca at the hospital after school. Blake drove, and we arrived at the hospital just after 4 P.M. Rebecca had been moved, so we waited for her dad to come and get us since we didn't know what room she was in and the nurse wouldn't give us her room number.

We followed her dad to her room, which was located in the psych ward. Before we went in, her dad spoke to us in hushed tones outside her room. He said that some of her memories had come back but that she still was experiencing some head trauma. The swelling on her brain had reduced to near normal, and she was going to go home tomorrow. He thought it would be good to see a familiar face, but felt it would be better if Blake waited outside in the hallway while I visited her myself, alone.

His expression scared me a little, but I gathered my nerve and went into her room. It had been two weeks since the attack, and while the bruising had lightened quite a bit, her face and arms were still discolored and covered with yellow bruises and abrasions. Her left eye was still bloodshot, but the swelling had gone down most of the way. She was sitting up reading when I entered the room and she looked up when she heard me. Her expression flashed to fear for an instant before returning to normal.

"Hi, Rebecca," I said, stepping up to her bedside. I could see the tiny stitches above her left ear even though it was mostly hidden by the stubble of dark hair. Her ear still had some white surgical tape over the top part of it that I hadn't noticed before. I waited for her to say something, but she just looked at me.

After a moment, I broke the silence, "How are you feeling? Your dad says you're going home tomorrow."

After a few seconds, she answered, "I'm doing better, I guess. "Daddy says they'll release me tomorrow."

"Well, that's great," I said because I couldn't think of anything else to say. After another minute, I added, "Don't be worried about what you missed at school. I've been taking good notes for you."

She looked at me without really seeming to see me and said, "I'm not worried. Daddy said I'm not going back to school. I'm going to finish the year at home."

"Well, I can still come over and study with you on Saturdays."

She was quiet again for a moment before answering. It was as if she was having to take time to process everything I said before she responded. "That's okay. Daddy said I'm going to have private tutors come to the house."

"You can still come to the games," I said. "When you're ready," I added hastily. "I can pick you up and drive you," I added.

"Maybe," she answered without any enthusiasm in her voice. After another minute of silence, she asked, "Where's Blake?"

I thought for a second before answering, "You remember him? That's good. He's outside. Do you want to see him? He can come inside if you want."

"No, that's okay," she answered quickly. I remember him, but I'd feel better if he waited outside. I'm not…back to myself yet, and I'd just feel better if it's just you."

"That's okay," I quickly answered. "Just know that we both care about you and will do anything we can to help you."

The silence grew between us again as neither of us spoke for a few awkward moments. I was just getting ready to say goodbye when she whispered something that I couldn't quite hear. "I'm sorry, what?"

She looked down and away before repeating herself. "I said, it's all my fault. What happened to me is my fault."

I stood stunned into silence. How could she think anything that had happened was her fault? I wondered. "Of course, it's not your fault, Rebecca. You aren't responsible for any of this."

"Of course, it's my fault," she said louder. "I shouldn't have been out there alone." She broke into sobs and pulled her blanket up to hide her face.

I was at a loss for words. I wanted to calm her and make her feel better, to let her know that none of this was because of her, but I couldn't think of anything to say. She kept crying as I stood there, trying to think of something to say. I felt a deep heartache at her distress and wished I could take away some of her guilt and grief.

Finally, her dad poked his head in and said that visiting hours were coming to an end since it was nearly 5.

I turned to Rebecca who still wept behind her blanket. "Bye, Rebecca. I'll try to stop by the house this weekend and visit." Before I turned to leave, I thought of one more thing to say. I turned and called back, "I'll try to bring you some cookies from the student store when I visit." She didn't respond but kept the blanket pulled up, hiding her face.

Outside, Blake grabbed my hand and walked me to the door without saying anything. As he drove me home, a silence enveloped us as he waited for me to be the first to speak. I was filled with so much pain and anger that it took me a few minutes to speak. Finally, I turned to him and said, "She blames herself. How can she think it's her fault?"

"It's part of being victimized," he said. "It was that way with my mom. She blamed herself every time my dad beat her. After she was gone, I blamed myself for her leaving," he explained. "Part of the healing process is to learn she's not to blame. Rebecca is going to have to learn to release the guilt. It could take a long time for her to heal." I reached over and, grabbed his hand, and scooted over next to him on the bench seat of his old pickup truck. "You're going to have to be her friend--be there for her--even if she doesn't want a friend and doesn't want you around. This is something that won't go away overnight," he finished.

I leaned my head on his shoulder as he drove, marveling at his wisdom.

Halfway home, he asked if I wanted to get something to eat, but I was exhausted from the short time at the hospital and didn't think I could eat anything, so I apologized. He said I had nothing to apologize for and that he was proud of me for being such a good friend to Rebecca. He drove the rest of the way to my house, gave me a too-brief kiss goodbye, and drove off.

That night I had a difficult time sleeping. I kept tossing and turning while thinking about Rebecca. I tried to think of something to say to her the next time I saw her, but decided Blake was right and that I just had to be there for her and let her heal in her own time. I finally drifted off to sleep and had fitful dreams the rest of the night.

The next morning was Friday, and I got up extra early so I could read over the material that I had ignored most of the week. Most teachers liked to give tests on Fridays--a way of spoiling many kids' weekends, I suppose. I typically enjoyed tests, which I know makes me a bit of a weirdo, but I am who I am. I got ready, drove to school, and sat on the steps to the library, waiting for it to open at 7:30. Blake had told me not to be alone, but it was early morning, and I doubted anyone who wished me harm would be up this early on a Friday morning prowling the school for victims. Besides, I didn't want to live in fear all the time, I told myself.

I sat for an hour on the cold marble steps, studying and reviewing until Mrs. Young came at 7:30 to open the door. She stared at me as if it was the first time she had seen me waiting early, even though, until recently, it had been a common occurrence. Blake had told me he wanted to get in an early workout that morning, so he wouldn't see me until after the game because, during lunch, he had to meet with the coach to go over a couple new plays and introduce him to a college scout that would be at the game that night. He had made me promise to "be safe" and not wander off alone after the game this time.

I walked up the marble stairs through the open door where Mrs. Young was trying to get her keys unstuck from the lock in the door. "Good morning, Mrs. Young," I said as I walked past.

"Good morning, Ann," she mumbled, calling me by my mom's name as she had recently started doing.

I soon became absorbed in my textbooks as I often did and was startled when the bell rang for the first period. I quickly picked up my books and hurried to first period. The day flew by and I sat in the Quad by myself during lunch instead of going to the library again like I would have done in the past. Even without Blake with me, people kept saying hi to me as they walked by, and many stopped to ask how I was doing. Blake had said everyone at school knew me, but I still think most people were only stopping by because they knew I was Blake's girlfriend.

Near the end of lunch, Perla came and sat down right next to me and told me all about this weekend's parties, "Just in case I wanted to go to any." She seemed boisterous and happy today, and I was glad. As she walked off, I saw Rory walk up and start talking to her. They walked off separately, and it seemed like he was unhappy with whatever arrangement they had.

The rest of the day dragged on uneventfully. I usually enjoyed Fridays because of the tests, but I had begun to realize just how empty school was without Rebecca. I hoped she and her parents would change their minds about her not returning. After the 7th period I went home to get ready for the game that night.

I ate a snack, and then an idea struck me and I made a picnic dinner for after the game. I packed four sandwiches--three for Blake--some chips, three bottles of water, and for dessert, I found a box of animal crackers in the pantry. I figured this way, Blake and I could spend some time together alone without me feeling guilty for keeping Blake from eating dinner. As I headed back to school, I thought more and more about what tonight would be like. Every way I imagined it, it was going to be a very special night.

CHAPTER 17
NOW WE'RE EVEN

I arrived at school early. The lights in the parking lot were already on even though it was still light outside. The one working light in the tunnel shined dimly as I walked through, and all the stadium lights blazed brightly even though it was only 6 P.M. There was no JV game because their season had already ended, but still, the game wouldn't start for at least another hour. After fifteen minutes, I decided I should have brought a book to read until the game started, even though reading a book while waiting for the game to start would have marked me as a nerd. After another quarter of an hour, the stands started filling up, and it wasn't long before the band arrived and started warming up.

By the time the game started, it was dark. No moon was visible, but I wasn't sure if that was because it was a new moon or because the sky was overcast with dark clouds. Blake led our team out of the tunnel again, breaking through a paper banner and running to the center of the field to the enthusiastic yells and cheers of the crowd. I yelled right along with them wondering how I ever could have missed this much excitement the last three and a half years.

The other team got the ball first and scored, but Blake threw a touchdown pass on our first possession, so we tied it up right away. The rest of the first quarter stayed pretty close, with our team scoring another touchdown, but by the end of the first quarter, the other team scored both another touchdown and a field goal, which put them ahead of us. This was the closest game all year, and the crowd was on the edge of their seats, cheering or booing wildly.

By halftime, each team had scored another touchdown, which put the score at 21-25. We were trailing, but I wasn't worried. I knew Blake would put everything into the game in the second half.

After halftime, the game continued right where it left off, with our team receiving the ball, and within a few plays, Blake had run it into the end zone and we were ahead for the first time. Everyone was crazy with excitement. I was cheering along with everyone when suddenly I smelled cigarette smoke. I started to look around just as Joey and Kenny MacGruber sat down on the bench just above me. They reeked of cigarette smoke, and I could smell a strong odor of alcohol and sweat.

Joey MacGruber leaned down and smirked before saying, "Hey, Elizabeth." His reddish-blond hair was pulled back into a greasy ponytail and looked like it hadn't been washed in weeks. His dark shirt also looked like it hadn't been washed recently, and with the stadium lighting, it looked like it could have been either dark blue or black. It had several stains on it that could have been from previous meals or just from being so dirty for so long. He wore white tennis shoes that he put up on my bench right next to me. They, too, were stained and dirty. He took a drag from the cigarette he held between his thumb and forefinger and blew the smoke in my direction.

His brother, Kenny MacGruber, sat next to him, silent, but a similar smirk spread across his pock-marked face. His reddish-brown goatee was thin and patchy. He wore a thick gold chain over his Ridgecrest Wildcats school shirt.

I tried to ignore them and turned back around to face the field. Joey moved his feet so that they dug into my hip. I turned around and glared at him.

"Oh, sorry," he said with a mock apology before laughing. They were both tall, but sitting on the bench behind me made them tower over me even more, and it was difficult not to be intimidated by them. Kenny put his black booted foot on the other side of me and nudged it into my other hip before laughing.

I was trying to figure out what to do when a thick-heeled boot stomped down on Joey's shoe and foot to my right. He let out a yelp and pulled it back, glaring down at the person. I looked up to see Perla standing next to me. Relief spread through me, and I couldn't help but smile.

"Oh sorry," she said in her raspy voice, "but this seat is taken." She was wearing tall, thick soled boots that lace up to the top which was most of the way up her calves. It was a cold night, but she still wore short cut off jean shorts. She also wore a Ridgecrest Wildcats school shirt, but the top collar was cut off into a deep V and the shirt was very big on her so that I was sure Joey and Kenny had a good view down the front of it from where they were sitting and staring. She noticed where they were gazing and said, "Lissen, you don't want no part of this. I've got plenty of friends around here. Should I call them over to teach you two some manners?"

Joey elbowed Kenny and jerked his head to the left, and they stood up and walked off.

"Thanks, Perla. That was great," I gushed.

Perla sat down next to me and said, "Forget about it. Those guys are jerks. I used to know Kenny when he was on the team, but he started dealing and I kicked him to the curb. Don't get me wrong, I like to party, but there's partying, and there's letting things control you. Know what I mean?"

I nodded even though I wasn't sure I did. I wasn't sure what to say, so after a minute, I asked, "Are you here with anyone?"

She laughed and said, "Yeah, no, I'll decide who I'm here with later tonight."

Perla baffled me, but I decided I liked her. She was her own person, and she was comfortable with who she was. She was so different from me, but she seemed so happy and carefree that it was difficult to not like her, and as I returned my attention to the game, I relaxed again, and we enjoyed watching the game. She could scream and cheer as loud as anyone in the stands and I felt myself loosening up even more as the third quarter progressed.

At the start of the fourth quarter, the game was still close. We were ahead 35 to 32. Blake was always better in the second half of the game and he wasn't disappointing anyone.

I felt my phone vibrate in my pocket and pulled it out to see if my mom was texting me. I looked at my screen for a minute and reread the message. It said, "Meet me in the Quad." It was from Rebecca.

I knew Rebecca went home from the hospital, but I couldn't imagine her coming to the game. Not only because the memories would probably be too traumatic but also because she probably still needed to heal before her dad would have let her go out herself. Maybe she wanted to come here, but once she got here, she realized she couldn't handle actually coming to the game with all the noise and the memories of what had happened on the football field afterward. It didn't make much sense, but Rebecca didn't always make sense to me.

I didn't want to miss the rest of the game, but I thought about Rebecca waiting for me. I didn't want her to be alone and feel abandoned. I knew how difficult it must have been for her to even come this far, so I made up my mind. As I stood up to go, Perla looked up at me.

"Where you goin'?" she asked. "Want me to come along?"

I hesitated before answering. While I didn't relish the idea of walking in the dark to the Quad alone, I knew that Rebecca would feel a lot more comfortable if it was just me who came. She would probably feel betrayed if I brought someone else--like I had replaced her or something--even though that wasn't the case and didn't make sense to me. I wanted to make sure Rebecca was as comfortable as possible. She probably just wanted to tell me that she was doing better. I hoped that she would tell me that she was going to return to school.

I turned to Perla and replied, "No, I'm just going to meet a friend, but thanks."

She looked at me and smiled big. "Oh, I understand. I think I misjudged you."

I wasn't completely sure what she meant, but I didn't want to wait to have her explain. I grabbed my purse and started walking down the concrete stairs toward the exit tunnel. Before I turned and went through the tunnel, I looked out onto the field to see if I could catch a glimpse of Blake so that maybe he would see I was leaving for a few minutes and not look up into the stands and wonder where I had gone. Down on ground level, it was difficult to pick him out, but when I did, it was clear he was engrossed in the game, and I didn't want to distract him, so I walked the last few steps, turned left, and went through the tunnel.

I took a breath I didn't know I had been holding when I emerged from the tunnel. There were only a few people outside the stadium, waiting in line to go to the bathroom. I turned right and walked past them in the direction of the Quad. It wasn't a very far walk, but it grew darker as I walked away from the lights. By the time I got to the Quad it was so dark I could barely see. My eyes had still not adjusted from the bright stadium lights, and the combination of no moon, the overcast sky, and no lights made me practically blind.

I stepped over the curb and took a few tentative steps onto the grass. I could see dark shapes that I knew were trees, but it was so dark that everything I could see was in deep shadows. I wondered why Rebecca asked me to come here instead of meeting me in the parking lot or by the student store where at least there would have been lights. I knew she probably wanted to avoid people, but it still wasn't making sense to me and I was starting to become uneasy. The clouds broke just enough for a few stars to lighten the Quad enough for me to look around a little. There was nobody visible that I could see.

I had just decided I should turn around and go back when I smelled cigarette smoke. Kenny MacGruber stepped out from behind a tree with a baseball bat in his hand. Fear gripped me, and I quickly turned to run, but immediately ran into Joey MacGruber, who must have stepped up behind me. I screamed and started to turn away, but Joey grabbed me by the hair and yanked me off my feet and to the ground. I landed on my back with a thud, and the breath was knocked out of me mid-scream.

Joey looked down and sneered, laughing a choppy little laugh with half of his lip pulled down, holding a cigarette in his mouth. He turned to Kenny, still laughing and said, "I told you the phone we took from the fat bitch would come in handy." He took a drag off his cigarette as he said this, and ashes fell off the tip and floated down next to my face.

I couldn't scream; I couldn't even catch my breath. I was hyperventilating from the fall and probably from fear as well. Joey had let go of my hair when I started to fall and when I lay gasping for air, trying to get up, he started laughing. Kenny walked up from the other side of me and stared down at me. He put the bat against my face and pushed my face over to one side.

"I don't see what the fuss is all about," Kenny said. "I mean, there's a lot of girls prettier than you at this school. I just don't see what Blake sees in you."

I was still gasping but was starting to catch my breath. I opened my mouth to say something when Joey took a step toward me and kicked me hard in the stomach, driving the breath out of me again, and once more, I was wheezing and trying to take in a breath.

"We're going to do to you what we did to your fat friend, bitch," he taunted.

My fear turned to anger when he said this. I thought of Rebecca lying in the field alone, bruised and broken, and how she would never be the same. He stood towering over me. I rolled over onto my back, brought my foot up, and drove it into his crotch.

He let out a strangled squeal, grabbed his crotch, and dropped to his knees. I brought my foot back to kick him in the face, but before I could drive it into him, he dove on top of me, pushing my foot aside, straddled me, and slammed his fist into my jaw.

My eyes instantly watered, and things got blurry for a few seconds. When things came back into focus, Kenny was telling Joey to hurry up. Joey smiled and said, "No, I'm going to make this last. She's going to remember this for a long time. Nobody's going to disturb us out here. They're all at the game." After a few seconds, he took a drag off his cigarette and added, "Your turn will come." His forearm was resting on my throat, making it hard to breathe and impossible to scream. Suddenly, I heard footsteps running toward us.

"Hey, stop!" somebody yelled from a few yards away to the right. Joey and Kenny looked over, and I managed to turn my head enough to see Rory running up to us. I could see Joey smile as he looked at Kenny and nodded toward Rory.

Kenny just raised the bat and swung. Rory was running toward Kenny and the bat, and even though he tried to stop, his momentum carried him into the swing of the baseball bat. He tried to put an arm out to halfway block the bat, but the bat made solid contact with Rory's arm before bouncing off and hitting Rory in the ribs and knocking him down.

Kenny took a step toward Rory, but Rory scrambled backward and got to his feet before Kenny could take another swing. Rory took a few steps back, clamoring away, holding his left arm with his right.

He looked down at me and took another step back before muttering, "Sorry, Beth," and turning and running away into the darkness.

As I watched him scurrying away, I felt what Rebecca must have felt on the night of the Blood Moon-- helpless, hopeless, afraid, and utterly alone.

Joey started laughing again as he watched Rory stumble and run off. Kenny watched him go and called out to Joey, "Now you better hurry." Joey just grunted and replied, "Naw, he ain't nobody. He's just running scared."

I started sobbing. A fear overtook me, unlike anything I had ever felt. I felt so powerless and vulnerable. I struggled to move, but Joey just added more pressure to his forearm, and I almost blacked out from the lack of oxygen before he let up and moved his hand down.

He started unbuttoning my pants, and I fought to stop him. His left hand gripped my left wrist and held it down so I reached up with my right hand and half scratched at his face and half tried to drive my fingers into his eyes.

He grunted in slight pain and punched me in the mouth. My lips were smashed against my teeth, and I could taste the blood pouring out of my broken lips and into my mouth.

Joey kneed the side of my leg hard, forcing my legs apart, but then tried to yank my jeans down and couldn't. He struggled for just a few seconds and soon had my pants down past my knees. The stubble on his face felt like gritty sandpaper, and I could smell the combination of sweat, alcohol, and cigarettes wafting off of him. His breath smelled like a mixture of beer, old cigarettes, and moldy mushrooms. The smell before had been noxious, but now, from just a few inches away, the smell was nauseating.

I could feel his hand groping me, squeezing me. I squeezed my eyes shut, but that did nothing to lessen the humiliation and pain of what was about to happen.

Joey's foul breath was revolting and overwhelming as he turned his head and joked to Kenny, "You're going to like this one. She's putting up more of a fight than the last one."

A type of mania overtook me when he said this. I raised my head off the ground, opened my mouth, and bit his ear as hard as I could. He yelled and slammed his fist into my gut.

"Hey, how about some help here," he demanded. Kenny looked down and took a step toward us.

I turned to spit out blood, which was still pouring from my busted lip--and I hoped from Joey's torn ear. When I turned, I thought I heard footsteps racing toward us.

Without warning, Blake rushed toward us in his white and purple football uniform. Kenny raised the bat to take a swing, but Blake was too quick for him. He bent down as he ran and, in one swift movement, caught Kenny by the legs and dumped him on his head. Before Kenny could get up or do anything, Blake took a step toward him and kicked him in the face. I heard the crunch of what must have been Kenny's nose breaking when Blake's cleat smashed into Joey's face. Kenny lay on the ground clutching his face, moaning. Blake turned to Joey, and I saw the same fierce, angry expression on his face that I had seen the day I had stopped him from going after Joey and Kenny in the parking lot the day they had vandalized Rebecca's car. Now, there was nobody to hold him back, and his eyes held a deep rage.

Joey started getting off me while trying to pull his pants up. "Hey man, we were just having some fun. We didn't know she was yours." I pulled my leg back again and kicked him in the knee, knocking him down.

Blake smiled for a second before turning his attention back to Joey. Joey tried to scramble backward in a kind of crab walk while he simultaneously tried to get to his feet. He had just managed to get to his feet when Blake reached him and slammed his fist into Joey's mouth. Joey fell back down and scrambled up to his hands and knees before Blake took another step toward him and planted a kick square in his face and then another one in his gut. Joey rocked back and forth in pain, moaning.

Blake looked around as if searching for more opponents and then walked over to where I was still laying on the wet grass. I had managed to pull my pants up, but I was still shaking so hard that I doubted I could stand up. Blake knelt down beside me and asked if I was alright.

I wanted to answer, but I just broke down and cried. Blake helped me to my feet and held me until I finally started to feel safe again. He had rescued me from something too horrible to even think about.

I buried myself in his arms and held on tightly. I didn't want to ever let go.

I'm not sure how long we stayed like that, but Kenny and Joey were still lying on the ground writhing in pain when Rory walked back with Perla. Perla walked over and slammed a kick into Kenny's stomach, and he groaned again but stayed on the ground. Rory said the police were on their way and said that we should stay here--as if we would have gone anywhere. Perla came over and rubbed my back for a minute, telling me everything was going to be okay. I smiled at her, reaching over and squeezing her hand before burying myself in Blake's embrace again.

The police finally arrived and took Joey and Kenny away in handcuffs. Rory had to go to the hospital because his arm was probably broken. Perla said she would drive him so he wouldn't have to ride in an ambulance. Blake insisted that I ride in the ambulance, but the paramedics said he could ride with me. He phoned my parents on the way and told them to meet us there, but didn't give too many details--just that I was okay but that they were going to check me out to make sure.

I ended up spending the night at the trauma center because the doctor said he wanted to make sure I didn't have a concussion. My mom, dad, and Blake waited with me all night so I wouldn't be bored by myself since I wasn't allowed to go to sleep that night because of the possible concussion. It's not like I would have been able to sleep anyway. The adrenaline had left me very shaky, and I was developing a pounding headache from being punched in the jaw and mouth. In the end, the doctor decided I didn't have a concussion, but she wanted me to stay a few hours for observation anyway.

The events of the night had left a lasting impression on me. I had escaped Rebecca's fate but had a better idea of what she had gone through if not exactly at least an idea. I felt lucky but also guilty. I was saved because of Blake. Nobody had been there for Rebecca. I had not been there for her. I was determined to make sure I spent time with her every day, even if she was home-schooled. I would just have to change my afternoon routine to study at her house instead of the library. Mrs. Young would really be lonely without me, I thought.

I laughed when I thought this, and Blake looked at me and asked, "What?"

"Nothing," I smiled back at him. "I'm just glad you rescued me," I said.

"Well, now we're even," he said. My mom looked at him oddly when he said that, and for a moment, it looked like she was about to ask him about it, but thought better of it and just waited silently, holding my dad's hand and leaning her head on his shoulder.

It was four A.M. when the doctor finally came in and said we could go. We thanked her and started toward the parking lot. Since both Blake's and my car were at school, my dad asked Blake if he wanted us to drop him off on the way home, or if he wanted to sleep on our couch and get a ride home in the morning.

I smiled big when Blake said he would appreciate it if he could spend the night and go home in the morning. My dad looked at me, beaming at Blake and said as long as Blake understood that he was sleeping on the couch. My mom laughed and Blake assured him that he promised to stay on the couch.

We got home just after 4:30. As we walked up the sidewalk to our front door, Blake said, "Looks like you missed your curfew again, Beth." My mom laughed and said she'd let it pass this time. I gave Blake a quick kiss and went up to bed while my mom brought down sheets, a pillow, and a blanket for Blake to use on the couch.

Half an hour later, I still couldn't sleep even though I knew it would be light soon. Finally, I crept downstairs and lay down next to Blake on the couch. It wasn't a large couch, but we managed to squeeze together. I felt safe next to him and soon drifted off to sleep.

Chapter 18
Open Invitation

I awoke the next morning alone on the couch. I looked around but didn't see Blake anywhere. I debated going back to sleep, but the smell of waffles was a deciding factor in getting up. I walked slowly to the kitchen, still very sore from the previous night. I had a bruise on my left inner thigh where Joey had kneed me. My lip was tender, and I worried that it would split open again and start bleeding again once I started eating.

When I got to the kitchen, Blake, my mom, and my dad were all sitting around the table. My mom looked up and said, "Well, look who decided to join us. Good morning."

"What's that I smell?" I asked, not even bothering to respond. I knew I was being slightly rude, but after last night, I figured I deserved a sleep-in. My voice was raspy and hoarse, kind of like Perla's. My throat and neck were a little sore still from where Joey had held me down with his forearm.

"I talked your mom into making waffles," Blake answered.

"And I went out early this morning and got some strawberries to go on them because Blake said that's how you liked them," my dad added.

As I smiled, the scab on my lip cracked open just a bit, I grabbed a napkin to dab the tiny drop of blood I could feel forming. Blake stood up and said, "Here, Beth. Take my chair." He pulled it out and then went to the counter and brought back a big plate of waffles piled with strawberries and syrup.

"There's no way I can eat all this," I said, looking down at my plate, which had enough food for me to eat breakfast, lunch, and dinner.

"Don't worry," Blake said, smiling big. "That's why I'm here."

I took a bite of my waffles and strawberries. My jaw ached on the side that had been punched as I chewed, and I wondered how bad my lip and face looked. I could feel the swelling in my lip, and my jaw was definitely sore where Joey had punched me, but overall, I didn't feel too bad. The shakiness from the previous night had disappeared. My wrist was bruised where Joey had gripped it to hold me down, and my face was probably bruised, but considering what had almost happened, I felt lucky. Blake had rescued me. I took another bite and smiled as I chewed.

Blake watched me from across the table. "Aren't any of you going to have any?" I asked.

My mom laughed and said, "Honey, we ate a couple of hours ago. It's after 10."

"10:18," Blake said, then added, "Don't worry, I'll help you finish those off."

My mom looked at Blake and smiled, "I've never seen someone eat so much," she said.

"We should invite Blake over every Saturday," I said without thinking, then blushed.

Blake and my mom looked at each other before Blake turned and said, "Your mom already said I have an open invitation every Saturday morning for breakfast.

"Actually, Blake, you have an open invitation to eat here anytime, breakfast, lunch, or dinner.

He smiled his big crooked smile, picked up a fork, and reached across the table to grab a bite of my waffles.

"Hey," I said in mock protest. "I'm not done yet."

We sat in silence for a few minutes while Blake and I finished off my waffles. Something seemed off, but I couldn't think of what it was. Finally, I figured it out and asked my dad, "Why aren't you in the office?"

He replied, "It's Saturday."

"Yeah, but you always go to work on Saturdays for some emergency-something."

He looked over at my mom and said, "I've been thinking that I spend too much time at work. From now on I'm going to stay home on weekends. If I have to, I'll check in on my computer from home."

I knew he would still be working quite a bit from home on Saturdays, but it was a start. My mom smiled when he said this so I knew she was happy about it.

I ended up not catching up on any studying because Blake stayed the whole day. My dad actually didn't even get on his computer. We just sat and talked most of the day, ate, talked some more, ate some more, and then after dinner, my dad offered to drive Blake home--probably so they could have their own version of The Talk.

On Sunday, Blake drove over for breakfast again. As he ate I started thinking how my mom would soon regret the open invitation for free meals. After breakfast, Blake offered to drive me back to school to pick up my car. My mom said I needed to come right home afterward, so Blake followed me home, and we spent the day together again with my parents. I could tell my mom was still worried about me, but by evening, I think she was beginning to believe I was okay. My dad seemed to be making good on his promise because he spent the day with us in the living room and not in his home office on the computer. It was a great weekend. My mom didn't want me to go back to school on Monday but instead said I should take a few days off to recover. I laughed at the idea and was at school by 6:30 on Monday morning.

I went to the student store and bought a few shortbread cookies since I was supposed to go over to Rebecca's after school to help her study.

Chapter 19
Post Game

Rebecca ended up not withdrawing from school, but instead was put on home health status which meant she got to stay home and do all her work without going to school. A teacher from the school would stop by once a week and give her a packet for the upcoming week and then pick up the previous week's work at the same time. She and her dad had agreed that she would return to school to participate in the graduation ceremony. Blake and I had been spending a few hours on Saturdays at her house studying. She and I were also attending a Survivor's Therapy Group once a week. It was helping me deal with the fear and other feelings I didn't know I even had. It was helping Rebecca a lot. I was so glad Blake had suggested it to me and Rebecca's dad, Dr. Swartz. He said it had been helping him and his dad since they started attending a similar one, and I could tell Blake seemed so much more comfortable and relaxed lately.

Blake would come over for breakfast on Saturdays and we would head over to Rebecca's to study, but really, we would spend most of the time talking. Rebecca was slowly starting to return to herself. She was changed and would be forever--I knew that--but it was nice seeing some of her old personality return.

The routine of school continued, but things were different now. Blake and I ate lunch together every day in the Quad. Most students avoided us now because they were angry at Blake for leaving the game to rescue me. We ended up losing the game in the fourth quarter, 39-35. Since we were out of the playoffs, Blake now seemed to be the most unpopular kid in school. It was funny, though because people still would say hi to me when they walked by but would completely ignore Blake. They knew what had happened because the news spread through the school like wildfire, but Blake just said, "Some people take football too seriously." Joey and Kenny MacGruber weren't coming back to school anytime soon. Their friend Devon had gone to the police and said they had bragged about what they did to Rebecca. That, along with the attack on me, which was witnessed by Blake and Rory, meant they were going away for a long time. Even though Joey was 19 and Kenny was only 17, the district attorney decided to charge both of them as adults.

Two weeks after that night, Blake and I were sitting on the grass in the Quad eating lunch when Rory and Perla came over to where we were eating. Rory's arm was still in a cast and Perla looked like she was carrying his books for him. Perla sat down next to me while Blake and Rory went off to talk. I commented to Perla that it was nice to see her and Rory together.

"Yeah, we been together since that night. I ain't never been in a relationship this long before, but after what he did that night, I knew he was the one for me. No more playing the field. I found the right guy," she explained.

I smiled big and we talked a bit before Blake and Rory came back. After Rory left, I asked, "What were you two talking about?"

"He just asked if I needed him to watch you anymore. I told him he didn't need to. Now that football is over, I have plenty of time."

"I'm sorry you won't be playing football anymore," I said. "It must be hard to give up something you really love."

He looked at me for a couple of minutes before replying, "It's not as hard as you think. So I'm not the most popular kid in school anymore. So what? Football is just a game. It's not like I lost a person I love, like with my mom."

Blake had begun to open up and talk more and more about his mom. He and his dad were in a support group together, and Blake said that this time, he was actually hopeful things would work out.

"Besides," he added after a couple of minutes. "Who said I won't be playing football anymore?"

"What?" I asked, confused. "I thought the season was over."

"Beth, you need to think ahead. You're too stuck in the here and now," he joked. "I got an offer to play quarterback at the University. Full ride scholarship." He waited a few seconds, then added, "And I didn't have to spend every day in the library."

"That's great." I added hesitantly, "You know, that's where I'm going."

"I know. In fact, I was kind of counting on it. You might have to tutor me a bit here and there."

"Wait, when did you submit your application?" I asked.

"I didn't have to submit an application.

"Wait, you didn't have to submit an application? What about the SAT scores and the character essay portion? What did you write on that part, or did you not have to do any part of the application?" I demanded.

"I didn't have to fill out the application, and I didn't have to write an essay," he explained. "They made me an offer," he replied. "There was a scout at the last game, and he said he was impressed by my playing."

"But you left the last quarter. Most of the school is still mad at you."

"Yeah, but the scout said that showed more character than I could write in an essay or application, so they asked me to come play for them, and I said yes."

I sat quietly for a minute before Blake read me like he always did.

"What are you worried about?" he asked.

"Blake, I know there will be a lot of college girls there. Very pretty girls."

He looked right at me before taking my hand and replying, "Why would I need anyone else when I have you, Beth."

I smiled as I thought about how sometimes change could be good.

Extra Map and Schedule

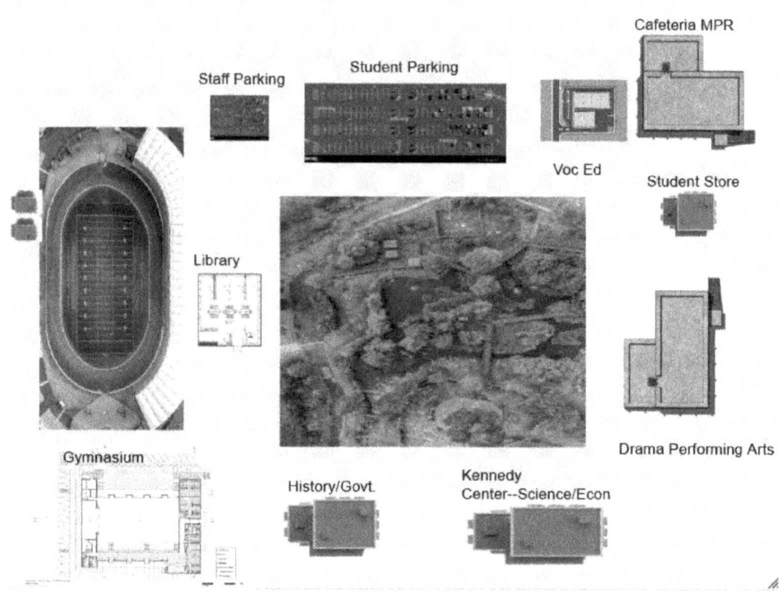

Elizabeth's schedule:

1. History/Government
2. Calculus II
3. AP English
4. Lunch
5. Science -Hart
6. Creative Writing
7. Study Hall because PE is optional Senior Year so she has a free period

Rebecca's schedule:

1. PE --had to make up PE
2. Science
3. AP English
4. Lunch
5. Calculus II
6. History/Government
7. Computer design

Blake's Schedule:

1. Algebra
2. Science
3. PE
4. Lunch
5. Economics
6. English
7. History/Government